MYST
ccR

A WATCHING SILENCE

A
WATCHING SILENCE

Anthony Masters

SIMON & SCHUSTER BOOKS FOR YOUNG READERS
Published by Simon & Schuster
New York • London • Toronto • Sydney • Tokyo • Singapore

SIMON & SCHUSTER BOOKS FOR YOUNG READERS
Simon & Schuster Building, Rockefeller Center
1230 Avenue of the Americas, New York, New York 10020
Copyright © 1991 by Anthony Masters
Originally published in England in 1991 by
Simon & Schuster Young Books under the title *Klondyker*
First U.S. edition 1992

SIMON & SCHUSTER BOOKS FOR YOUNG READERS is a
trademark of Simon & Schuster.

Designed by David Neuhaus.
Manufactured in the United States of America
10 9 8 7 6 5 4 3 2 1

Library of Congress Cataloging-in-Publication Data: Masters, Anthony
A Watching-Silence/by Anthony Masters.
        p.   cm.
Summary: After moving to a remote Scottish island,
Martin uncovers a mystery surrounding the disappearance
of valuable antiquities.
[1. Mystery and detective stories. 2. Islands—Fiction.
3. Scotland—Fiction.] I. Title.
PZ7.M423875Kl   1992
[Fic]—dc20 92-3519 CIP
ISBN: 0-671-79173-7

To Robina, Mark, Vicky, and Simon—with much love

One

The ruined village was the most unearthly place Martin had ever seen. The five stone cottages—crofts, the locals called them—had no roofs left to speak of, and were built in a rough semicircle, facing the dark water and a beach of black rock. It seemed to be at the very end of the earth, a totally primitive place, full of pitted driftwood and seaweed, with the sun a cold red orb in a vast sky of scudding cloud.

It was all very somber, and when the wind came, as it often did in mid-October, the crofts faced a vicious, boiling sea that hurled flotsam and jetsam into the cove, piling it up on the beach throughout the winter. Martin loved the place, loved the melancholy of it all, and he came to the village for comfort. He could feel the echoes of the past and the presence of the long dead. Now, at sunset, the complete silence was broken only by the faint sighing of minute waves on the pebbles.

Lost in his own thoughts, Martin heard the stirring, scraping sound and discounted it. It was probably some small creature, maybe even the odd rat. But then he heard it again and again in its own regular pattern, and he came to with a jolt. What was going on? He was standing where he usually stood—on the black rock-strewn beach, imagining what the tiny community had been like a couple of hundred years ago. The noise seemed to be coming from the farthest of the buildings, whose four roofless walls reached raggedly to the sky. It was positioned on a promontory that ran out toward the sea, and the sound was repetitive—stirring, scraping, stirring, scraping—surely too repetitive for an animal.

Slowly, the hairs rose on the back of his neck and a chilly fear uncoiled in the pit of his stomach. Supposing—just supposing—the sound was human?

Slowly and unwillingly, Martin walked over the rough boulders until he reached the peaty mound of the foreshore. He had never considered himself brave, but then, he had never really been challenged. There had been the occasional bully at school whom he had usually avoided, a big dog that had once chased him and lost interest, a wood he had walked back through at night—or, rather, had run through. And since they had come to Shetland, there was only nonacceptance and loneliness. Nothing to really frighten him. Not until now.

The sound continued regularly, almost rhythmically. Then it stopped—just as Martin reached the gaping hole between the stones that had once been the front door of the croft. Total silence. And it was only Martin's imagination that told him it was a watching silence. Wasn't it? He stood there, rooted, not wanting to move, while the great cold northern sea stirred uneasily behind him.

Then he turned away and walked rapidly back to the beach, slipping and stumbling as he went, conscious of the perspiration standing out on his forehead despite the chill of the late afternoon. While his back was turned, he heard a slithering and a rattling and then silence. He didn't dare to turn around, yet he had an overriding feeling that someone—something—was coming soundlessly down the beach toward him. Forcing himself, Martin turned quietly. The crofts looked back at him, hollow, alien, menacing.

He almost laughed aloud. What was the matter with him? What was getting him down? Of course—he knew. Ever since he had left Indiana with his ornithologist parents and his sister, Clare, he had been lonely and miserable. He hadn't made friends at the

big school at Lerwick. Most of the children had been
born on Shetland or the surrounding islands and he
just didn't fit in. His sister already seemed to have
loads of friends, but then, everyone said she was
much more outgoing. Perhaps he found it especially
hard because he knew they were only there for six
months while his parents wrote a book. And now,
because he was alone so much, he was hearing
things. It was ridiculous. He waited, and the silence
was heavy and foreboding. Then an overpowering
urge came over him. He had to go and look in the
croft—just to reassure himself that he was not going
crazy.

Martin had been in the house before; indeed, he
was rather fond of the place. There was nothing left
but the four walls and a cellar that smelled of seaweed. This was partly exposed, as a section of the
old stone floor had dropped into it. Even in the fad-
ing light he could see into the cellar now. As he stood
there, something caught Martin's eye, and he leaned
over in curiosity to see exactly what it was.

The object gleamed sharply up at him, but in the
darkening shadows of the setting sun he couldn't
make out its shape. There was only one thing to do,
he realized grimly: He would have to go down into
the cellar and find out for himself. The prospect
wasn't pleasant, but he knew he had to do

it for the sake of his own curiosity and pride.

Reluctantly, Martin trudged around to the back of the croft, his feet sinking slightly in the peaty soil. This was the only way down to the cellar, where the old stone steps had crumbled away and there was a smell of earth and sea. He had been down there in daylight but never as the sun set, and the tiny settlement seemed more inward-looking, more darkly magical than ever. But his feet were already on what was left of the steps, and he hurried down into the dim interior.

It was there on the floor, still gleaming, and now he could see its shape. Martin was staring down at a long silver knife with an intricately carved handle. It was in beautiful condition and certainly didn't look as if it had been buried in some nook or cranny of the croft. Someone had exerted loving care on the knife; they must have polished it every day, he thought. As to its use, he didn't know. It seemed too long for a letter opener, but it certainly wasn't a weapon. Either way, it shouldn't be lying there. He remembered the scuffling sound. Could someone have been here? Were they watching him now? Waiting for him?

With a sudden, fearful action, Martin grabbed the knife and ran back up the broken stairs.

There was no one around, and he wandered back

to the beach, suddenly fascinated by the light of the last dying rays of the autumn sun as they shone into a boggy pool at the water's edge. He knelt down beside it, staring into the sunshot translucence. A small crab stirred lazily and, as if in some dark mirror, he fleetingly caught a glimpse of his own reflection. Wide-open face, freckles, soft ginger hair, but with a hint of determination in his blue eyes. It was strange, looking at himself like this, almost as if he could see beyond his features, deep into his mind. As he watched, he clasped the silver knife and then shivered. Without thinking he held the knife up, and it glowed darkly, powerfully. Then it seemed to flicker, and he saw crimson blood running down his finger. It dripped into the pool and spread—red smudges on the blackening surface.

How could it have happened? How could he have cut himself? It all seemed quite impossible. Suddenly, the last ray of sun disappeared and the tired red orb slid into the ocean horizon with a last blinding flash. For a few seconds there was a glimmer of purple and then the beach seemed dark. A gusty, chilling wind blew up, rattling loose stones in the crofts and sending tufts of dried moss scudding into the air. Then it was gone and there was silence.

Martin sucked his finger; the blood tasted salty and metallic. He examined the knife, but apart from its brilliant shine it was quite inanimate. He must have twisted it against his finger—somehow. He stood up, wanting to go home. He'd take the knife with him and see what his parents felt. No doubt they'd tell him to take it to the police station and that would be that.

Martin walked back toward the bumpy track that led to the summer house his parents were renting on the shore of the loch. There were seals and otters there but not much human company and, as today was Saturday, Martin was looking ahead to another rather lonely day tomorrow. He knew his mother and father were concerned about him, but there seemed more or less nothing anyone could do about it. He didn't fit in—and that was that.

Sucking his finger, he grabbed his bike, swung a leg over, and began to pedal slowly home.

The thing sprang out of the hedge at him with a grunt and a snarl, and in seconds Martin braked sharply and flew straight over the handlebars. He landed hard on his shoulder, his feet entangled in the bike. When he looked up, he shrank back in shock and terror. What faced him was some kind of monstrous travesty of a creature: a huge cat's head with its features wildly exaggerated, and a gray sweat-suit body and limbs that he could only just make out in the gloom.

He was frozen, staring up, unable to move, hardly able to breathe, watching the nightmare creature while it watched him. Then it leaned over him, and he saw a gray-gloved hand outstretched. Instinctively he knew what it wanted. The silver knife. He hesitated and the hand reached nearer.

"Okay," he breathed. "Okay." Pulling the knife out of his sweater pocket, Martin handed it over. The knife was grabbed with a grunt of satisfaction and the thing bounded off. When it had gone, Martin lay there, shaking. Of course it wasn't a monster, he reasoned. It was a man—or a woman—with a cat's mask. But why? Out here, in this wilderness? Could he have just had some kind of joke played on him? No. There was the knife and he was sure the knife was valuable. He continued to shake as the word "cat burglar" came into his mind. But it was a term used to describe an agile thief. Cat burglars didn't dress as cats—or have cat masks.

Still trembling, Martin tried to pick himself up and fell down again immediately. He'd forgotten his legs were still tangled up with the bike. Painfully, he managed to extricate them and then he got to his feet more successfully. He didn't seem to be hurt—just shaken up and terrified out of his wits. He mounted his bike and began to pedal as fast as he could. Where was the cat man now? he wondered. Around the next bend, waiting for him again, or had he got what he wanted? He was going uphill now, but he didn't feel in the least tired and his legs were feather light as he pumped the pedals. As Martin crested the hill, he picked out a fleeting figure approaching a parked car. It was the cat man—Martin recognized his slim build in the gray sweat suit immediately. He didn't glance back, but even so, Martin came to a grinding, shuddering halt.

A full moon had risen and in its pallid light Martin watched the cat man get into the car. A few seconds later it sped off. The vehicle was distinctive—a small Russian car, a Lada, its license plate obscured by mud, perhaps deliberately, Martin thought. The Lada was soon lost to sight in a bend in the hill and Martin pedaled on, the shock easing as he coasted downhill. So the cat man had a car. Or could it be a cat woman? Tears ran down his face suddenly, and he felt a great sense of relief as all his pent-up emotion spilled out. He could see the loch where his parents lived, and its sudden welcoming familiarity made the tears come harder. The glow of light, the pale moonlight on the loch, the sound of a dog barking somewhere, all seemed to make him feel deliriously, deliciously safe.

Martin's parents were horrified when they heard

Martin's story. His father was tall, thin, and often silent. He was an international expert on birds and was in the Shetlands studying the habits of a rare species of gull. His mother was the opposite—talkative, excitable, imaginative. She was an ornithologist too, but specialized in illustrations. Clare, three years older than Martin, had inherited her mother's characteristics and talents and would soon be bound for art school. Martin was more like his father; he had a lot of inner resources and could be equally silent. But he *did* like people—and right now he wanted masses of them.

"You mustn't rove around alone like that," said Mrs. Fuller. She was given to wearing long print dresses that covered her ample, big-boned frame. She wasn't exactly fat, but her clothes were tentlike.

"Mom—I like going there."

"Then we'll all go there as a family," she began, but Clare interrupted.

"It's weird," she said.

"What is?" asked her father.

"A man like that. Prowling around. Dressed up as a cat. He must be crazy."

"We'll try the police," said Mrs. Fuller. She went out and could be heard dialing.

"This knife," said his father slowly. "Describe it again."

Martin did—as best as he could.

"I remember something about that." Mr. Fuller went over to a bookshelf. The house was a converted croft, a summer house used by a family in Lerwick, but it had been rented to the Fullers for the fall and winter.

As he searched, Martin wondered if he should tell his father that the knife had turned on him and cut him. He thought about it a bit and then decided not to. After all, it had probably been only his imagination.

Meanwhile, his father was riffling through an old book of Shetland folklore. "Got it."

"What is it, Dad?" asked Clare, munching her way through an oatcake.

Anywhere the Fullers went, Mrs. Fuller would ensure they ate local produce, local food, local everything. "Our bodies should be a part of the place," she had reminded them all again when they arrived on Shetland. Martin hadn't been so sure this time, for he hated the salted porridge his mother occasionally produced.

His father laughed. "There was the winged knife in the Fairy Hoard—it's an old Shetland story. A Norseman stole some precious metal belonging to the Little Folk and disguised it as knives and plates and silverware and . . ." He talked on for a while as

Martin turned off, Clare yawned, and Mrs. Fuller came back from the phone.

"They're sending someone up," she said, and began to clear away the dinner things, making a good deal of clatter.

Neither Martin nor Clare was interested in what their father was saying, and their mother seemed to be too worried about what had happened to Martin to care about some old story. What could all this have to do with the cat burglar? Martin wondered. But he couldn't shake out of his mind the way the knife had seemed to turn on him.

"Now, here's something interesting," said his father. "A set of gold and silver objects reputed to be made from the Fairy Hoard is on show at the Lerwick Museum—I wonder if it still is. This book is about twenty years old. I'll give them a call tomorrow. I know the present curator. He's an archaeologist—now, what's his name? Oh, yes, Dr. West. Now, he—"

"It's Sunday tomorrow," Clare interrupted mournfully. "They won't be open." Although she had quite a good social life on the island, she couldn't wait to leave Shetland. "Back of beyond," she continually called it—and that was the politest thing she said. Unlike Martin, Clare couldn't see the wild, rugged magic of Shetland. Back of beyond

would have been a compliment in Martin's eyes—
and so would the ends of the earth.

"So it is." Mr. Fuller smiled ruefully at his daugh-
ter. Martin glanced at his sister. She was a beautiful
girl, with the same wide-open face as his own, but
without the freckles. Instead, she had tumbling
auburn hair like her mother's, and her skin was clear
and slightly tanned.

"You can ask Magnus, though." She smiled affec-
tionately at him. Magnus worked on the island's
roads during the week and put out lobster pots on
weekends. He was in his sixties, an islander, and a
mine of local information.

"I might," said Mr. Fuller enigmatically.

Clare turned to scrutinize her brother. "You look
awful," she said. "Awful."

"Thanks for nothing."

"Shouldn't you go to bed?"

"I'm waiting for the police."

"I'm sorry, Martin, really I am." Clare's voice softened. "We should do more things together. I do care.
Really I do."

Martin knew she did. For all her brisk manner and
for all his father's academic interests, he knew they
were both shocked and frightened by what had happened. And as for Mom—even now she was looking
at him as if he might pass out on the floor.

Two

The policeman came up from Lerwick. He was middle-aged and sharp. "Officer Haydn," he said as he shook hands and, refreshingly, came straight to the point. "You sure you're okay—would you like a hospital checkup?"

"I'm fine."

"So I hear you had a nasty experience over at Settler?"

Martin told him exactly what had happened, and he took copious notes. When Martin had finished, Haydn said, "We'll go out and have a look tomorrow morning. I know the old croft you mean."

"What do you think's happening?" asked Clare, who never beat around the bush.

"Couldn't tell you. Doesn't make any sense to me at all."

"No robberies recently?" asked Mr. Fuller.

"Not of antiquities. Not of anything like that

knife." He looked longingly at the door. "I'm sorry the boy had a scare. Could have been one of the locals. Those Ladas are quite popular here—what with the Russian klondyker crews coming in and wanting to pick up spare tires for their own use back home. Pity the boy couldn't see the license plate." Again he gazed longingly at the door. "We'll look into it tomorrow and get back to you."

When he had gone, Clare said, "We won't hear any more from him."

Martin knew she was right.

He slept lightly that night, troubled by dreams of leaping gray cats and a village full of kittens. They, too, were gray and they occupied each house, mewing piteously. Eventually, Martin woke halfway through the night to hear thunder growling and sheet lightning crackling over the hills. As the thunder came nearer, he got out of bed to watch the storm and heard the wind mounting, moaning and tugging at the surface of the loch, whipping the dark water into bursts of spume. Only a mile away lay the sea, and as the wind heightened, he thought he could hear the waves crashing on the shore. Every so often the lighthouse gave out its plaintive warning and, occasionally, the loch was lit by lightning, making the water and peat and rank grass and foreshore look like a waterscape from the beginning of time.

Martin stayed by the window, watching the storm until it began to peter out toward dawn. He felt oddly comforted by the furor outside, viewed from his warm window. He enjoyed seeing the elements clashing, as if they were expelling his frustration and fear and anger at the way he had been used by the cat burglar. Like the storm, Martin wanted to lash out, to fight someone, to prove he was not some kind of wimpish dreamer.

At five he went back to bed, for the storm was spent and growling and his bed was luxuriously inviting. Martin soon fell into a deep, dreamless sleep until he was awakened by his mother at ten.

"There's been a shipwreck," she said. "Didn't the storm wake you?"

He shook his head.

"You must be so tired, darling. I almost came in, but I thought if you *were* asleep . . ." Her voice trailed away.

"I slept fine," lied Martin, and sat up. "What's this about a shipwreck?"

"One of those klondykers," she said. "Gone up on the rocks at Settler. Where that terrible thing happened to you."

"I'm going down there," he said, jumping out of bed. Despite his interrupted night, he felt good—

alert and refreshed and full of energy. His bad experience seemed to have been blown away by the storm. Forget the cat burglar—let him or her get away with it. And forget the silver knife and the tricks his imagination had played on him. He would go to see the klondyker.

But his mother had different ideas. "You're staying here," she said grimly. "And having a nice quiet day." A long argument broke out which ended in a compromise. He was to go with Clare, and that was the end of it.

"Supposing she doesn't want to go?" said Martin hopefully.

"She will," replied his mother grimly.

They cycled hard toward Settler. They had both gotten used to klondykers since they had come to Shetland. They were the rusty, down-at-heel workhorses of the North Sea, the factory ships that canned fish from the trawlers, added tomato sauce, slapped labels around the cans, and then sent them on to the stores. Most of the klondykers came from Eastern Europe—Russia, Poland, and Lithuania— and Martin often saw their sailors in Lerwick, going in and out of the bars, watching movies in the run-down old theater, and taking spares back on board for their Lada cars from the yard that specialized in collecting them. He had often wondered about the sailors, about what kind of life they lived on the rusty hulks and what kind of life they lived back in their own countries. But this ship, according to his father, who had already been down to Lerwick to get a Sunday newspaper and the gossip, was Nigerian and called the *Saturn*.

Martin and Clare turned the bend and scrambled over the rough, peaty ground to Settler. The ship looked enormous. For once, the beach was crowded with sightseers and the five crofts looked diminished, unimportant. The *Saturn* loomed over the beach, pinned to the rocks a few yards out into the water. It was a horrendous sight, battered and with its plates buckled, slewed at an angle. A few seamen were on deck.

"What a wreck," said Clare with excited pleasure.

But Martin felt a strange sadness. It was a rusty old hulk anyway, and now this had happened. The *Saturn* had originally been painted blue and white, but what with the gouts of rust running down its side and half the name faded away, it looked a very sorry sight indeed. Washed up, thrown there by the giant hand of the storm, the *Saturn* looked as if it were there all too permanently.

"What are they doing?" asked Clare of one of the local farmers.

"They're going to try and refloat it on the next

high tide," he said, adding with a gloomy relish. "But I don't reckon it'll take."

"Look," said Martin. "Here comes Dad with Magnus."

They were walking slowly down the path to the beach, staring at the *Saturn* just as Martin and Clare had—in surprise and wonderment. They were pointing out the keel and the propellers sticking out high and dry from the sea that was now flat and calm again.

Magnus was a very striking man. He was tall and of immense breadth, with blond hair and a blond beard. He looked very Nordic which, as Dad had pointed out, was how he should look.

"These people aren't Scots," his dad had said when they first arrived. "They're Nordic. Norsemen—at least some of them are." And most of the islands and place names were in Norse too—Fetlar, Papa Stour, Foula, Burravoc, Yell, Ulsta, Mousa, and so on. Some of the old Norse words were also used, like *fell* for hill, *garth* for farm, *holm* for small island, and *voe* for a sea inlet. Dad had been right; it was a foreign country here all right—a mysterious place. And the most mystical man in it was Magnus himself. He took part in all the Viking longboat celebrations, when a model boat was made and then burned on the sea, after which a great party was held. For his work with the lobster pots, Magnus often used a canoe and, when the weather was calm—or even when it wasn't—he paddled around the island, slipping in and out of the coves and around the great lumps of rock that stuck out of the sea.

"Martin! Clare!" Magnus came across to them, grasping them both in a big bear hug while Mr. Fuller followed behind, whistling tunelessly. "I hear you had some trouble."

"I'm okay now," said Martin quickly.

"I asked Magnus about the Fairy Hoard," said Mr. Fuller. Martin could see that underneath his reserve, his father was worried.

"*Do* you know anything about it, Magnus?" asked Martin curiously, his thoughts temporarily dragged away from the fate of the *Saturn*.

Magnus shrugged. "It was always called the Fairy Hoard, though that's only some old myth. But the collection was valued at thousands. The museum at Lerwick was a damn silly place for it, I suppose, although it was kept in a safe. The curator's been there for too long. I've always blamed William West for being so complacent. Said there were no thieves on the island. Well, that was disproved. It was stolen ten years ago, and never found. West and most other people believed it had been taken off Shetland. But I was never so sure," he added darkly.

"Who gave it to the museum?" asked Martin.

"It was found by a farmer in the early part of the century. Turned up when he was rebuilding a pigsty."

"Maybe the fairies stole it back." Clare grinned.

"Maybe they did," Magnus smiled gently at her. "I'd like to think that they had. But unfortunately, I think it was villains—maybe local villains."

"Was anyone caught?" asked Martin.

"No. But there was a hell of an argument about the lack of security. West almost lost his job."

"They couldn't sell it, surely? It's unique," said Clare.

"Only on Shetland."

"Then whoever stole the Hoard must have taken it off the island," said Martin authoritatively, and his father, who had been listening to the conversation between Magnus and his children with interest, nodded approvingly.

"Do you know exactly what was in the Hoard, Magnus?" he said.

"Not exactly," Magnus replied. "Of course, Dr. West would remember far better than I—"

"What do you think about this knife Martin found?" asked Clare eagerly.

"Well, I thought it might be—" Magnus looked worried.

"Have you told the police?" she said. "Surely they should be alerted? It could be really important."

"I called them." He smiled ruefully. "I don't know whether they believed me or not. As I imagine you've gathered, I'm known as a bit of a mystery man around here. I'd have been the local witch if I'd been born a woman. I also spoke to Dr. West, but he claims the knife you described, Martin, is nothing like the one in the Hoard. And I can't remember the detail."

"Why don't the police search the crofts?" demanded Martin.

"They did—early this morning. But they didn't find anything else."

"Maybe they were distracted by the sight of the *Saturn*," said Clare, her gaze on the hulk on the rocks.

"Maybe," replied Magnus.

"We should search ourselves," said Martin. "Shouldn't we, Magnus?"

He nodded. "Not a bad idea—the beach is a bit busy at the moment though." He paused. "There's something else I came up with." Magnus seemed unwilling to go on.

"Well?" asked Martin impatiently.

"It's only an old story," Mr. Fuller put in cautiously.

"But what *is* it?"

"As your father says, it's an old story. I didn't know it myself. I dug it up out of one of the folklore magazines. I wouldn't take it seriously, or get scared or—"

"Magnus," said Martin. "Please!"

"All right, then. It's to do with Settler, but nothing to do with the Hoard, as far as I know. There was an old woman here who was reputed to be a witch. And she was burned. The people hereabouts believed she brought disease to their cattle and sheep—even to themselves. The usual thing. Just before she died she cursed them all, saying she'd live on eternally through her cat. And Settler would die." Magnus looked around at the ruined crofts. "I suppose in a way her curse worked. Eventually."

"Are you saying this person running around with a cat mask on is the reincarnation of the local witch?" Clare laughed scornfully. "I suppose at a pinch they could be trying to scare off people from searching Settler, but, if so, all they're doing is drawing attention to themselves. Whoever it is must be a real idiot. Driving off in a car and everything. What a jerk."

"It was frightening in the dark," protested Martin.

"Anyway, there'd be no need for that," said Magnus quite sharply. "Settler has been haunted for years. No islanders will go near it."

"But a person in a mask—" started Clare again, scoffing.

Her father intervened. "He or she gave Martin a terrible shock—enough for us to insist he not go to Settler alone. So the cat's been effective. Any more instances of anyone being warned off?" he asked Magnus.

"No, not to my knowledge. But I told you," he insisted, "no local would go near this place anyway. At least, not until the *Saturn* put in an appearance."

Martin felt a sense of loss; he knew his father wouldn't let him go near Settler—at least not around sundown. Maybe he could negotiate, and get permission to come down in the early morning. "Aren't the police going to try and catch the cat?" he asked hopefully.

Magnus shook his head. "Officer Haydn seems to be seeing the cat as a local dressed up."

"Pinching a piece of the Hoard?"

"He doesn't seem sure about that either," replied Magnus. "They just don't believe the knife has anything to do with it."

There seemed to be an atmosphere of total inertia at Settler. The people on the beach stared at the ship and the crew; the crew stared back at the people on the beach. High tide came and went, and the *Saturn* remained firmly where it was.

"They'll have to get a tug now," said Magnus, "or it'll be in danger of breaking up."

"Won't they have to pay salvage?" asked Mr. Fuller.

"Yes—it's going to cost."

"Anyway, we must be going." Their father was brisk now.

"I'll need to get my pots set." Magnus turned away from the *Saturn*.

"Can we stay, Dad?" asked Martin. "There are lots of people around, and it's only one-thirty."

"Only if you both stay together and come home before it gets dark."

"Okay," Clare groaned.

"Having a treasure hunt?" asked Magnus.

"That's what I was frightened of," replied Clare. "Bet we don't find a thing."

They didn't, although they both spent a couple of hours rooting through the ruined crofts. They attracted little attention, for most people had drifted away.

Martin spent an hour in the cellar where he had found the silver knife. There were a few loose stones but with nothing behind them except peaty mold. He also examined the floor, but it didn't reveal anything.

Spotting yet another loose stone lower down in the wall, Martin tried to pry it out. As he did so, a shadow fell on the ground behind him. Thinking it was Clare, he didn't bother to look up.

"I've nearly finished," he grumbled. "Give me a while longer." When there was no reply, he looked up irritably and then jumped back in shock. A dark face was looking down at him thoughtfully.

"Sorry to startle you."

"It's okay."

"I couldn't resist coming over to have a look and see what you were up to. The skipper said I could take a walk," he added, as if justifying himself. "I saw you and the girl poking around. Looking for buried treasure?"

"Just—exploring," said Martin self-consciously. "Are you from the *Saturn*?"

"Sure. My name's Ali."

"Do you come from Nigeria?" said Martin curiously.

"Yes." Ali's voice was sad. "It seems such a long way away. I don't even know whether we'll ever get back home again."

Ali leapt down into the cellar. He looked seventeen or eighteen, lean and well-built, with shining ebony skin. Martin thought he could detect a note of real desperation in his voice.

"How did you go aground?" he asked.

"We were outside Lerwick and the anchor dragged. Then one of the engines broke down and we ran aground. There's a tug coming tomorrow, but I don't think we stand a chance. Those rocks have gouged a big hole in the *Saturn;* they've got the pumps going day and night."

"They'll get you back even if the ship doesn't make it," said Martin. He suddenly felt a liking for Ali. He came across as someone who said exactly what he was thinking.

"You don't know our company," Ali said. "They're mean as blazes."

"But they couldn't *strand* you here," insisted Martin.

"No? That's what you think."

After that there didn't seem much to say. Martin was sorry for Ali, but he still couldn't believe that his company could be uncaring enough to strand him forever. And what would the British government have to say about it?

"Why don't you come on board?" asked Ali suddenly.

"I've got to get back before dark," replied Martin.

"Don't you want to look around?" Ali sounded wistful, as if he were as desperately in need of company as Martin was.

"Well—yes." Martin wondered what his father would say. But he didn't wonder long, for he was sure he would say no. Very firmly no. But the offer was attractive; he would love to look around a wrecked klondyker from Nigeria. Who wouldn't?

"The local people here, they're inviting us to a party. In the—café, is it? Or—"

"Pub?"

"Pub—yes. I have to stay and look after the ship." Ali sounded empty and lost.

"Whatever for? No one's going to steal it," said Martin, smiling.

But Ali didn't seem to understand the joke. "The skipper—he's frightened of looters."

"There won't be any up here." Martin was sure of that. But the more he thought about the offer, the more he wanted to accept it. To go on board this mysterious old ship that had come all the way from Africa would be incredible. Then he had an idea. "Who's organizing the party, Ali?"

"A big man, with a large head and—"

"Magnus. My dad's bound to be going, then. Maybe he'll take me there and pick me up afterward. What time could I come?"

"They leave the ship at eight—"

"I could come for an hour perhaps. I wouldn't be allowed to stay long."

"I don't want to be alone." Ali was plaintive now.

"What are you afraid of?"

"It's this village. It's full of spirits."

"Nonsense." But Martin knew exactly what he meant.

"I can only ask."

"I don't know why you want to go on the rotten old ship anyway."

"Clare, it's come all the way from Africa."

"So what?"

The conversation rambled on as they cycled home. But when they arrived, Mr. Fuller's reaction was surprisingly positive. "I've already met the skipper and he's said anyone can go on board—in small groups, that is. Coming, Kate?"

She shook her head. "I've got work to do tonight."

"Clare?"

But she wasn't interested either. "So it's just you and me, Martin."

Martin nodded. Somehow he was disappointed, although he was determined not to show it. He would have been much happier with just Ali. Ali would forget all about him once Dad started looking around and asking questions. Maybe—Martin stopped himself from thinking. At least they were going on board. At least he had met someone at last who had actually said he wanted his company. Despite Mr. Fuller's presence, Ali beamed at both of them as they hailed him from the beach. It was dark now, with the huddle of ruined crofts in a semicircle around the *Saturn*. They couldn't see its rusty, battered hull; instead, it looked like a fairy-tale castle that had magically arrived at Settler. It was lit all over, bathed in a warm glow from the portholes, and there were little pinpricks of color on the decks and superstructure.

Martin and his father hurried up the gangway, and Ali met them at the top.

"I am very pleased you have come," he said. "It is not good here alone." He looked across at the darkened crofts. "Bad spirits."

"They were good people who lived there," Mr. Fuller said. "Good, simple people."

But Ali was not to be challenged. "Bad spirits," he repeated. "I know—from back home." Without waiting for a reply, he began to show them around the klondyker, first belowdecks, where all the gutting and cutting, cleaning and cooking and canning, went on. In contrast to the outward appearance, the interior of the *Saturn* was scrubbed clean. Every bulkhead was painted an intense white, while almost every surface seemed to be made of shiny stainless steel. It reminded Martin more of a hospital than a factory ship. When they had inspected store-rooms, the crew's quarters, and the engine room, Ali led them back on deck and eventually to the radio room and the bridge. He obviously knew a great deal about the running of the *Saturn*, and he explained it all with great enthusiasm.

It was only when he made them coffee in the galley and his father said "Now I'd like to ask a few questions" that Martin asked if he could look around the decks alone. He wanted to think about Africa, not listen to a torrent of questions. Ali and his father told him to be careful over and over again, and then, finally, they let him go out.

Martin stared out into the darkness. There were a few lights on the hillside, but nothing else. He could be anywhere—even in Africa, looking out from the *Saturn*, after having sailed thousands of miles across the sea. Ali and Martin. Senior officers. Maybe Ali was captain and he was the first officer. They worked in harmony, in friendship. They were good mates, experienced seamen, explorers—and now the African continent was in front of them, despite the chilly Shetland air. They were going to explore together.

Martin wandered around the deck until he could look out to sea. He imagined that Shetland was somewhere bleak and far away and that the *Saturn* was tied up in some steamy African anchorage.

Walking around toward the port side, Martin almost bumped into a dark shape—some large object shrouded by a tarpaulin. He stared at it vaguely for a while, his mind still immersed in his African fantasies. Then his curiosity prompted him. What could it be? A piece of machinery? A lifeboat? But all the lifeboats were clearly displayed, among the few neat and trim-looking items on the *Saturn*'s decks. His curiosity grew, and Martin pulled at one side of the tarpaulin to reveal a wheel and a bumper. It was a car. And there was something familiar about it.

Martin pulled the canvas up higher. He felt tense, suddenly afraid of what he might find.

"What's up?"

Martin cried out in alarm. He dropped the tarpaulin and, whipping around, saw that it was Magnus. He was smiling, but there was something set, almost rigid about his smile.

"What are you doing here?" Martin asked abruptly, not really knowing how rude he sounded.

"I came to look for your dad," he replied gently, the smile widening more naturally. "I want him to come up to the party. We're having a rare time."

"He's in the galley, drinking coffee. Ali's just made us some."

"And who's Ali?"

"I don't know. He's like the cabin boy or something. He invited us on board. The skipper said it was okay."

"I'm sure it's fine. But I thought I'd pick up your dad—I know what he's like when he starts asking questions."

They both stood and stared at the tarpaulin until Martin realized he must be behaving strangely and moved away.

"You coming?" asked Magnus.

"Where?" asked Martin vaguely.

"The party."

"No. It's all drinking. It'll be boring."

"Your dad will run you back, then."

"I—"

"Something wrong?" There was a slight edge to Magnus's voice.

"I was going to stay and talk to Ali."

"Another time. I'm sure your parents would want you safe and sound at home after what happened last night."

"Yes," said Martin resentfully. He was sure they would. But why was Magnus being so protective? His father was here and could decide for himself. Also, it was strange that Magnus had come all the way down to the ship when he had already asked

Dad to the party—and presumably Dad would have gone there eventually. Stranger still, however, was what lay under the tarpaulin. The wheel and bumper were enough to make him reasonably certain. It was a Russian Lada and he was sure it was the one the cat burglar had driven away in.

"Come on, it's getting late," Magnus was saying, but Martin couldn't contain himself any longer.

"What's under this tarpaulin?" he blurted out.

"That's the chamber of commerce presentation."

"What?" Martin's mind seized up. Why should the chamber of commerce give the *Saturn* a Lada? His brain whirled, looking for an explanation.

"The *Saturn*'s been coming over to Lerwick for many years now and, as you probably know, it's the only Nigerian klondyker we've got. So we asked them what Nigeria could use—and they said they could always use more tractors. We raised the money and we got them one."

A tractor, thought Martin. With a wheel like that? "Is it a special one?" he asked.

"Very special."

"What—"

"Come on now. Let's go and get your dad."

"Okay." Martin followed Magnus reluctantly, his mind buzzing with questions.

He *had* to have another look. While Magnus was

being introduced to Ali, Martin said that he must have dropped some money on the deck. His father nodded impatiently when he said he must go back and look for it. Mr. Fuller was still full of questions he wanted to ask Ali about the *Saturn* and he certainly hadn't welcomed Magnus's interruption. His father was the most enthusiastic person Martin knew, and when it came to new ideas and new discoveries, he was almost childlike in his eager interest. Martin loved him dearly for it, even if it was a bit of a drag sometimes. But Magnus had given him the most extraordinary look when he had asked if he could go back—a look full of anger and accusation, even of threat. But then it had gone as quickly as it had come, and Martin was not really sure that he had seen it at all.

Back on deck, Martin ran as fast as he could toward the tarpaulin, for he was sure, absolutely sure, that Magnus would follow him. As soon as he arrived, he pulled up the other side. Sure enough, another identical wheel, another identical bumper. Neither could possibly belong to a tractor. He yanked the tarpaulin harder and it came up a bit more at the back. The license plate was covered in mud. It was the same Lada all right. For some reason Magnus, the man he had come to know so well—and like so much—was lying.

Three

Martin woke early. When he looked at his watch it was 5:30 and the first streaks of dawn were lightening the enormous expanse of sky he could see from his attic bedroom. He wouldn't need to go to school for at least three hours and he felt absolutely wide awake. Last night he had been so tired that he had slept dreamlessly, without thinking about the Lada at all. Neither had there been a chance on the way home, to tell his father what he had seen, because his father was so absorbed in telling Martin what he had drawn out of Ali. "It's fascinating," he had said. "Life on those klondykers. I mean, I wouldn't mind spending a bit of time—a voyage—"

Martin had known there was no point in trying to tell his father anything then, when his enthusiasm was at its height, and now Martin wanted to think—to think about what he was going to do next—and he knew that couldn't be done in his bedroom. He wanted to be out, on his bike, with the wind blowing in his face.

He jumped out of bed and opened the window. There wasn't any wind, but the sharpness of the air stung his face. He *had* to go out. He grabbed a piece of paper and a pencil and scribbled a note: "Dear Mom and Dad. Can't sleep, so I've gone for a bike ride. Back in time for breakfast."

Martin crept downstairs, put the note on the kitchen table, and carefully unlocked the door. It was a wonderful morning—fresh and sharp and clear, with a tang of the sea. He dragged his bike out of the shed and rode away, feeling as vibrant as the morning itself.

He would tell his parents about the Lada over breakfast. That was the first thing that Martin decided. The second was that he would say nothing about Magnus; he must have imagined his hostility. After all, he had been incredibly tired. And the tractor business could just be a mistake. After all, why on earth should Magnus know exactly what was under that particular tarpaulin? He'd probably just been guessing.

Martin pedaled on, and before he had even realized it, he was speeding down the hill toward Settler. He jammed on his brakes. There was a bit of a mist in the cove through which only the radio mast of the *Saturn* poked. It was not a shifting mist but a dense, impenetrable one, and while Martin stood staring down, it seemed to thicken protectively. As he stood there, he felt an overpowering urge to go down. After all, his parents had forbidden him to go there only at night, not in the early morning—and he certainly wasn't afraid. So why was he hesitating? Was it the *Saturn* or the ruined crofts that were attracting him? Or a combination of both? He didn't know, but he wanted to get down to Settler. Fast.

As he sped down the hill, Martin continued to wonder what he was doing, why he was so deeply attracted to the ruined settlement. Was it because he was so lonely? Did Settler give him an imaginary life? Did the *Saturn* give him the same, with its exotic hint of a faraway continent? Or was it his new friend Ali who, although taken over by his father last night, had seemed so eager to get to know him? He couldn't really work it all out, and before Martin could give it further thought he was bumping over the soft, peaty shoreline.

The mist seemed to deaden all sound as Martin put down his bike and began to walk toward the crouched, roofless buildings that reared up at him through the gloom.

Now that he was there, Martin didn't know what to do, and when he looked at his watch he saw that he still had an hour before he would have to ride back home. He plodded on indecisively, until the hull of the *Saturn* loomed up through the mist and he was among the ragged stone walls of the crofts. Suddenly, a sound reached him. At first he couldn't identify it, but then he realized it must be the soft splash of oars.

Instinctively, he crouched down and watched. The rowboat was out of sight, but he could dimly pick out the gangway of the *Saturn*. At first he was certain that there was no one there; then he was sure he could see a man, watching, waiting for someone. The sound of the oars continued for what seemed ages and then stopped. For a while there was silence and the man on the gangway raised a hand in greeting. Then he heard what must have been the soft rubbing of a dinghy hull on the spongy seaweed. The dull thud of oars being shipped followed and, after a few seconds, another shape appeared on the gangway. There was a whispered discussion he couldn't hear and then the two men walked down to the shore, presumably to the beached dinghy. They emerged with what looked like boxes and proceeded to carry them on board the *Saturn*. This went on for about ten minutes while Martin, crouched in his watching position, began to feel the first signs of a painful cramp. Gradually it got worse and he could hardly bear it. He had to move.

When he did, it was so painful that he gasped, but neither of the two men loading the boxes so much as glanced up. With great relief Martin settled down again, the pain slowly easing. Then he whipped around. He was sure he had heard something move.

It had been a footfall. Soft. Catlike. Then he heard another—just a whisper of sound. Martin began to shake. He could see the cat gliding toward him. No longer a cat burglar, but a slim, long, ragged slip of an animal emerging from one of the crofts. He couldn't believe it at first; the mist was distorting shape and substance. But no—it was a cat all right. Flea-bitten and unpleasant to look at; thin, with its eyes as old as the hills. It was coming straight toward him.

Martin could bear it no longer. He broke cover with a cry of sheer terror. It was blocking his path, lips curled in a snarl, a row of small yellow teeth bared. The cat gave a guttural meow, turned, and streaked off toward the *Saturn*. Shivering, Martin watched it go like a bullet up the gangway just as the two men, still indistinct in the mist, were bringing up yet another box. He heard one of them curse, but rather than flattening himself again on the ground, Martin ran as fast as he could toward his bike. Then he pedaled like mad for home.

Over breakfast he told his parents and sister exactly what he had seen. He left out the information about Magnus's odd behavior—which he had already decided wasn't odd behavior after all. He also left it out because his parents, and Clare were not nearly as impressed or alarmed as he thought they might have been. He also decided not to tell them about the cat.

"You're making a drama out of all this," his sister snapped. She was never much good in the mornings, and Martin's latest adventure only seemed to irritate her.

His mother was dismissive. "I don't know what they were doing, but I *do* know *you* shouldn't have been there. How *could* you have gone snooping, Martin, after all we said?"

"But you said not to go down there at night."

"That's willful misinterpretation."

"Dad—"

"And don't go appealing to him," she said angrily while Clare looked triumphant.

They're all against me, thought Martin gloomily.

Thank goodness he hadn't told them about the cat. No doubt Clare would have killed herself laughing, and even Mom might have joined her. But what about Dad? He hadn't said anything yet.

Eventually he spoke, "It's strange about the boxes—"

"Oh, for goodness' sake," began Mrs. Fuller, "haven't you got anything better to do than—"

"I think I'll call the police. Have a word with Haydn."

"Oh, well"—she thumped down some toast—"have it your own way. Now—eat up, Martin. You might as well try to get some energy for school, however much you've already squandered on that wretched cove."

When Mr. Fuller came back, he looked disappointed.

"I got Haydn."

"What's he say, Dad?" asked Martin eagerly through a mouthful of toast.

"Apparently, they were loading up food. They were running out of supplies."

"At that time of the morning?" But, judging from his father's face, he knew he was clutching at a straw.

"They're expecting the tug, and the skipper hopes it'll be dragged clear."

"What about the damage?"

"They think they can limp, or be towed, around to Lerwick, but it'll take a while. There'll be no chance of taking on supplies until they get there. And those boxes were donated."

"By the chamber of commerce?" asked Martin.

"How did you know that? Yes. It was a gift like the party. I must say, this disaster is definitely bringing out the best of Shetland hospitality and generosity."

"Was Magnus involved?" Martin's voice was cool.

"Probably."

"You got something against him?" asked Clare shrewdly, studying his expression with interest.

"No. He's all right." Martin got up. He wanted to go. His father's explanation was probably right. And maybe he *was* making a drama out of it all, as Clare said. But he wanted a drama. Badly.

"By the way, Martin, I met the curator of the museum last night at the party—Dr. West."

"Oh, yeah?"

"I've invited him to dinner. He knows a lot about the island and may have some more things to tell us about the Hoard. He's looking forward to meeting you."

"Great," said Martin.

"You don't sound pleased," his father said in a hurt voice.

"Let him be," said his mother impatiently. "Can't you see he's worn out—though it's all his own fault."

Martin left the house with an ache in his heart. He had never felt so miserable. Even his new friend, Ali, would be leaving today, and he'd probably never see him again.

At recess Martin usually found himself wandering around the school playground alone. He had tried to join in the spontaneous games of soccer and, although he had been tolerated, he was never passed to and eventually gave up. There was nothing hostile in the other boys' attitude; it was just as if he weren't there, as if he were invisible. He knew that Clare, despite her early morning moodiness, was worried about him, but as her friends didn't have any younger brothers, there wasn't much she could do to remedy his lack of social life.

But today there were no games. The pupils stood around talking avidly, but each time he sauntered over to a group, they seemed to stop. Then he noticed that the old boiler room, at the very far side of the playground, was half open and a discreet, wary group was gathered at the door, watching something that had all their attention. Curious, Martin walked over, but before he could see what was going on inside, an older boy came over to him.

"Scram."

"What's going on?"

"Go away."

"But—what's everybody staring at?" Martin insisted.

The boy was big, and his expression was hostile. "This is island business. Get lost."

"Why can't *I* be part of the island?" Suddenly Martin's fatigue and isolation collided, and he realized he was close to hot and angry tears. He knew he should go away, but he couldn't. Unexpectedly the big boy's face softened.

"What's your name?"

"Martin Fuller."

"You from America?"

"Yes, my parents are ornithologists," he blurted out. "We're just here for six months." There was a break in his voice and the boy smiled at him sympathetically. "No one will be friends with me," Martin ended bleakly.

"Aye—we're clannish here."

"It's not fair." The tears were not very far away.

"No," he agreed. "It's not. But you won't like seeing what's going on here. It'll win you no friends."

"What *is* going on?"

"Someone's been naming."

"Naming? What's that?"

"A boy called another boy's father a name."

"And so?"

"They're slugging it out."

"In there?"

"In there," he said softly. "It's not nice."

"Who are they?"

"West and Dunglas."

"West—" Martin paused. "Isn't he—isn't his father the curator of the museum?"

"I think he is."

"And Dunglas—that's Magnus Dunglas's son?" He vaguely knew him—a big, wiry wild boy of sixteen or more.

"That's him. So you do know people." The big boy grinned.

"No, I don't. Just their names. Why are they fighting?"

"I don't know." His eyes seemed to cloud over and Martin was sure that he *did* know. "Now, get away. Don't hang around."

Martin turned away, his angry tears forgotten. West and Dunglas. Fighting. Why?

"By the way," said the big boy.

"Yes?" said Martin, turning back.

"I help run the Youth Club. Why don't you come to a meeting?"

"Well—"

"Make some friends."

"I might."

"Make sure you do. Thursday evenings. Seven o'clock."

"Okay." Martin moved away. The big boy was kind after all, and he'd think about the Youth Club. But meanwhile, his mind was otherwise engaged.

Four

There was no further reference to the fight Martin hadn't seen, and nothing broke the calm, routine waters of the schoolday. He didn't see either of the combatants and, as he biked home, Martin wondered if anything had really happened at all. Yet what were they all looking at if it wasn't a fight?

Martin always took a shortcut on his way home from school, which meant leaving the long, thin ribbon of a road that wound its way over the hills, overlooking a valley and, farther out, the cold, gleaming sea that shimmered like molten silver in the afternoon light. He would ride down a narrow, badly surfaced road and then onto a track that led past Magnus Dunglas's cottage and outbuildings, on toward the modest stone house that his parents had rented on the shore of the loch.

As Martin turned onto the track, he almost hit a rangy-looking man with a mustache. He wore an old parka and was smoking a battered-looking pipe. Martin skidded to a halt in a shower of loose earth and apologies.

"That's all right." The man, who was in his early sixties, smiled vaguely. Then he looked at Martin more astutely. "Aren't you Martin Fuller?"

"That's right."

"The young man who thought he'd found a piece of the infamous Fairy Hoard?" He gave a dry laugh. "Your father was telling me all about it. I'm Dr. West from the museum."

"It must have been important," replied Martin. "Someone in a cat mask stole it from me." He felt rather indignant at being patronized.

"Yes." Dr. West looked anxious. "That must have been a very unpleasant experience. It's never happened on the island before."

"It was probably only a local—so the police say."

"Yes, I'm sure it was. Some idiot playing up the legend. Tell me about the knife again. Try and describe it as accurately as you can."

Martin told him, and Dr. West shook his head. "It sounds interesting, but it's definitely not part of the collection that was stolen from the museum."

"Do you think that's off the island now?" asked Martin.

"Goodness, yes. It was obviously a gang from the mainland. I had the Hoard under what *I* thought was very tight security. However, do drop into our museum when you're passing. You'll find it fascinating."

"Er—yes."

"We're having a major rebuilding soon—an appeal raised thousands."

"That's good," said Martin politely.

"Are you proceeding down this track?"

"Yes, I was—"

"Then please don't be alarmed. You'll find my son a bit farther down. He's been in a fight with another boy at school, and now he's insisting on taking it further. I've done my best to dissuade him. I can't do any more." Dr. West gave Martin a little nod and walked away.

Martin rode on, but about a hundred yards from the Dunglas house, he saw the wheel of a bicycle sticking out of the grass and, a few yards farther on, a half-concealed figure that didn't move.

Martin stopped, curiosity turning to fear. There was something incredibly sinister about the lack of movement. Was the person hurt? Asleep? Dead? He should go and investigate immediately. But instead, Martin stood there indecisively and it was only with the utmost reluctance that he finally laid down his bike and walked slowly toward the body.

The boy was lying faceup, his nose badly swollen and a livid bruise on his cheek. Of course, Martin thought. This must be Dr. West's son. Why on earth had his father just walked away, leaving him in this state? The boy was tall and strongly built. One of his eyes was blackened and Martin thought he could see dried blood in his fair hair. Still hesitating, Martin knelt down beside him and gently shook him. Nothing happened until he shook much harder. Then, with amazing speed, the boy sat bolt upright and opened his good eye. He blinked and groaned, and blinked again.

"Who the hell are you?"

"Martin Fuller. I saw you lying there. You're hurt. I just met your dad."

"Of course I'm hurt." His voice was husky. "But I had him—whatever my father thinks."

"Who?"

"Peter Dunglas."

"What's your name?"

"Eric West."

"You were the ones who were fighting at school, then?" said Martin tentatively.

"You bet we were."

"Who won?"

"It should have been me," he reflected. "I suppose it was pretty even when the bell rang. If it hadn't rang, I'd have got him."

"Why were you fighting?"

"Family." His voice lowered. Then Martin noticed he had something in his hand. It glinted and glistened and Eric made a clumsy attempt to conceal it. Martin stared in amazement. It was the silver knife he had found in the ruined croft—the silver knife the cat burglar had taken away from him when he'd pushed him off his bike. Could Eric be the cat man? If he wasn't, how come he had the knife? Had he shown it to his father? And if he had, why hadn't Dr. West mentioned it? All these thoughts flashed through Martin's mind in a matter of seconds. Then he realized that while he was staring so intently at the knife, Eric was staring very intently at him.

"What's that for?" Martin eventually managed to ask.

"It's my knife." His voice was dull.

"Isn't it dangerous? To hold it like that?"

"I need it for protection."

"Where did you get it?" Martin changed the subject quickly. There was a quiet, unyielding desperation in Eric's voice that he didn't like.

"It's mine."

But Martin could contain himself no longer. "I found it."

"You?" Eric put his hand to his eye and winced.

"It was on the floor of the ruined croft. At Settler."

"*You* found it there?" He was incredulous.

Martin suddenly blurted it all out. "There was someone with a mask. A cat mask. I was taking that knife home. Not to steal it, but to give it to the police. And then—the person with the cat mask knocked me off my bike and took it."

"I see." It was obvious that Eric believed him now. He stared at Martin thoughtfully. "So that's what happened. Well, it wasn't me who knocked you off your bike."

"I didn't say it was. Have you shown the knife to your dad?"

"Not likely—he'd take it off me for the museum."

"He already knows about it."

"Does he? Well, he won't know I've got it, will he?"

"No," said Martin dutifully. "Where were you going?" he said suddenly.

"To the Dunglases'."

"Why?"

"Unfinished business."

"You wanted to go on fighting?"

"I haven't finished with him yet."

"You were going to fight with the knife?"

"No."

"Where did you get it?" Martin persisted.

"I found it at school."

"At school?" Martin was astounded. "Why was it there?"

"I don't know." Eric paused and then continued quickly. "One of the little kids had it. I heard him boasting to his friends that he'd found it in a box in the boiler room, and there were other things in the box. But when we went to look, the box was gone."

"Maybe he was lying."

"No. He was too scared of me to lie," said Eric, and Martin believed him. "Anyway, it definitely wasn't his, so I confiscated it."

"Your father says the knife's not part of the Hoard—the collection that was stolen."

Eric shrugged. "If that's what he says—"

"Is the knife what the fight was about?"

"Peter Dunglas. He said I'd taken it from the kid. But that's not what the fight was about. He's been needling me for months."

"What about?"

"His father, Magnus. He says my dad was care-less. Said he didn't look after the museum properly," he added.

"Why's he so interested in something that happened such a long time ago?" asked Martin.

"I don't know. Dad and Magnus have always been rivals for some reason I just can't understand—could never understand. He's traced his family back to the Dowains, and we can trace ours back to the Mikles—"

"Who are they?"

"Old Vikings—Norsemen who knew the Little People—Norsemen who stole the Hoard and turned the gold and silver into objects—bowls and jugs and flasks and cutlery. And my silver knife. I'm sure of it, whatever Dad says."

"And you and Peter were fighting over all that?"

"He's always saying things about my dad now. It really gets to me." He paused. "Dad's gentle—buried in his books and bits and pieces. He's not like Magnus, the famous man of action. And this knife business—Peter went balmy." He paused and rubbed his eye again. "The bell rang, and we hadn't finished. I *want* to finish."

"When did you find the knife?"

"Today."

"The police will want to know," said Martin hesitantly.

"I'll hide it somewhere. I'm not parting with it."

"Do you believe in the Hoard? That it originally came from the Little People?"

"No way," Eric scoffed. "But I'm not going to have Dad's name being taken in vain — having mud slung at it by the Dunglases. Peter and that father of his, they think they know it all. It's as if they own the island. The weird thing is that we see such a lot of each other. Dad's treasurer of the island chamber of commerce, and Magnus is secretary, you see."

"Suppose your father is wrong — that the knife is part of the collection."

"So?"

"If the knife turned up, then the other stuff might be around."

"But where?"

The solution came to Martin in a flash. "Maybe it's on the *Saturn*."

Eric stared at Martin in amazement. "What are you saying?" he asked eventually.

Martin began to explain about the boxes and how he had been told they were food donations from the chamber of commerce, just like the Lada that was lashed and tarpaulined on the deck of the *Saturn*.

Eric listened with growing interest. "So you think —"

"I think the boxes had the Hoard in them," said

Martin eagerly, warming to his theory. "Suppose the Hoard was never taken off the island . . . ?"

"Dad says that's impossible," said Eric.

"What if he's wrong?" replied Martin.

Eric said nothing.

"We should search the *Saturn*," insisted Martin.

"Oh, yeah? And how do you propose to do that?"

"I've got a friend on board. Ali."

"Who?"

"Ali's a bit like a cabin boy. We could go now."

"And search?"

"Take a look around anyway."

"Suppose Ali knows what's going on?" Eric asked suspiciously.

"He can't. I mean, he wouldn't have asked Dad and me on board if he knew they had something to hide."

"If you're right, I'm surprised the skipper agreed to any visits."

"Maybe he thinks it's better to be open, even if they have got the stuff hidden away somewhere on board. Though, of course, the boxes weren't on board then," Martin added reflectively.

"There's only one drawback to our scheme," said Eric.

"What's that?"

"They were meant to be trying to refloat the ship today. Suppose they were successful?"

"It's going only as far as Lerwick," replied Martin firmly. "I reckon I can still get on board. But it would be easier at Settler," he added.

Eric got painfully to his feet and put the knife in his saddlebag.

"Let's go," he said.

"Aren't you going to finish with Peter Dunglas?"

"You bet I am. But he'll keep."

They rode down the track on their bikes, speeding up even more as they passed the Dunglas cottage. They stopped briefly at Martin's house, where they found Mr. Fuller writing up some notes in a sheltered spot by the kitchen door.

"This is Eric," said Martin briefly.

"Hello, Eric. Been in a war?" asked his father, staring at Eric's battered face.

"Er—" was all the response he got, but Martin quickly answered for him.

"He got beat up by a bunch of bullies, Dad."

"I didn't think the school was like that."

"It's not, Dad. This was an—exception."

"Mmm," said his father vaguely. "So where are you off to now?"

"Look at the ship—if it's still there."

"It is," said his father. "I've been down to see it. They didn't manage to refloat it."

"That's a shame," said Martin, trying to conceal his relief. Eric stood awkwardly beside him. "Does that mean it's stuck there permanently?"

"I met the skipper—very nice man called Kinlata—Marbu Kinlata. They're bringing in a bigger tug tomorrow. He hopes that will do the trick."

"We'll go down there," said Martin.

"And you'll be back before dark?"

"You bet."

"Nice to meet you, Eric," said Mr. Fuller as the boys prepared to depart. "You ought to put something on that face. Witch hazel all over that cheek, beefsteak on that eye." He laughed uneasily and Eric laughed uneasily with him. As they rode off, Martin wondered if his father believed the story about Eric's face. Probably not. But at least he hadn't stopped them. For the moment Martin was just grateful for that.

Settler was deserted when they arrived, and the sky was a swollen gray with darker clouds coming in from the sea.

"Storm," muttered Eric. "That could do the ship in."

"How long away?"

"An hour maybe. No longer."

"We haven't got much time, then," said Martin. He shouted Ali's name, but he didn't come. Instead, an older Nigerian came out on deck.

"What do you want?" he said politely.

"Ali."

"He's not well."

"Can we come on board and see him?"

"There's a storm coming up," said the man. "Wait a minute. Here's the skipper."

Marbu Kinlata was well dressed, with a blue sweater, dark trousers, and a peaked cap. He was distinguished-looking, with an aura of authority. Martin's heart sank.

"Can I help you?"

"I wanted to see Ali, but I gather he's ill," gabbled Martin.

"He's got a fever." Kinlata's voice was crisp, but he didn't sound unfriendly.

"Can't we see him?"

"Are you Martin?"

"Yes. And this is my friend Eric."

Kinlata nodded. "He's spoken a lot about you. But there's a storm coming up, and we've trouble enough already."

"Just for half an hour? Eric says the storm won't happen yet, not for an hour."

"He's a weather prophet, is he?"

"He's an islander."

"So that explains everything." Kinlata smiled. "All right. Come and see him for a short time. He could use some cheering up."

As Martin and Eric ran up the gangway toward him, Kinlata, like Martin's father, began to comment on Eric's face.

"You fighting a war, young man?"

"School gang," muttered Eric.

"Here? I thought—"

"Will the *Saturn* really be in danger?" Martin risked the interruption and Kinlata seemed to accept it.

"It could be the end of it, if it's driven any harder against the rocks. . . ." He looked worried.

"But what will you do?" asked Eric. "In the storm. Will you stay on board or—"

"None of us will be heroes, I assure you of that. At the first sign of trouble I'll be putting the men ashore."

"They can stay with us," said Martin. "At least, I'm sure some of them can."

"I know they'll be welcome into our homes." Eric was very confident. "If anything goes wrong tonight," he added.

"That's good of you, and Mr. Dunglas has assured

me of the same. I believe he'll be down here later. We may have to shift stuff—"

"Unload cargo?" Martin fished.

"Just bits and pieces." His voice was enigmatic. "Now—if you want to see Ali, you'll have to be quick. I want him cheered up; he'll have work to do if this storm breaks." He paused. "And did you know he's also my nephew? I'm very fond of him and I have responsibilities to his mother."

"We'll cheer him up."

"I'm sure you will," said Captain Kinlata.

"Ali."

"Who is it?"

"Martin—with my friend Eric." Martin looked across at Eric rather anxiously, and Eric smiled.

"I'm not well." Ali's voice sounded lifeless.

The cabin was small and stuffy. Ali lay on a bunk, his face glistening with sweat.

"I've got a fever," he said. "I've had it before." He sounded utterly dejected.

"There's going to be a storm tonight," said Martin. "You may have to be taken off."

"Where will I go?" He was suddenly glassy-eyed with fear.

"You can come and stay with us."

"Yes?" Ali looked a little relieved.

"But you never told me about the skipper," said Martin accusingly.

"What about him?"

"That he's your uncle."

"Who told you?" whispered Ali.

"He did."

"He's *not* my uncle."

"But—"

"He says he is, but he's not." Ali was still whispering but very fiercely.

"Then who is he?"

"He took me from my father," said Ali evasively.

"But why?"

"To work here for nothing. As a slave. He'll never pay my fare home if the ship sinks—and neither will the company."

"We'll help you," said Martin reassuringly. He didn't know whether to believe him or not. There was something so naive about Ali that he could have been a younger brother.

"Ask him," hissed Eric.

"Ask him what?"

"Ask him about the boxes," said Eric impatiently.

"Oh, yes. Ali, there's some cargo aboard. We think it may belong to the museum at Lerwick."

Ali's reaction was electric. Despite his fever, he sat straight up in his bunk. "*What?*"

"Cargo. Boxes of precious metals. If they are here, they shouldn't be on board. They were stolen from the museum at Lerwick. Ages ago. But now someone's trying to get them somewhere. And we're pretty sure they're on board here. If the ship sinks—"

"There's nothing here." He was clearly very alarmed and the sweat intensified on his forehead.

"Ali—"

"If there was anything here, I'd know." He had stopped whispering and his voice was shrill.

"But you must know. Under the tarpaulin, that's no tractor. It's a Lada—a Russian car—used by—"

"No!" he shouted.

"What?" Martin stared at him in mounting fear. He glanced at Eric, who looked confused and indecisive.

"Go and look. You're crazy. It's a tractor. It was given to us by the chamber of commerce."

"I looked last night. It's a car," snapped Martin.

"You're crazy," repeated Ali, shivering. "Right out of your mind."

"Look," said Eric. "Why don't I stroll down—take a quick peek, and settle all this?"

"Okay. But be careful," said Martin, wondering if he sounded absurdly melodramatic.

Eric walked purposefully away, and Ali lay back

in his bunk. The sweat was really pouring off him now.

"Why do you say these things?" he accused Martin, his big, dark eyes fixed on him in suspicious fury. Martin felt a sense of loss; Ali would never be his friend now.

"Because I was attacked—and things are happening. Eric found a knife at school."

"A knife?"

"It's part of the Hoard. It was—" Martin stopped in mid-flow. How could he explain all this to Ali? It did sound crazy.

"Hoard? What's a Hoard?"

"It doesn't matter."

"But you are saying we have things on board we shouldn't."

"Yes." He was interrupted by a rumbling of far-away thunder and Eric's return. "See it?"

"Martin—"

"What's the matter?"

Eric was looking puzzled. "Under the tarpaulin—"

"Yes?"

"There's a tractor."

"What?"

"A tractor. Not a car. A tractor."

Five

Martin stared at Eric unbelievingly. "Don't be silly."

"It's true."

"I'll look for myself," Martin blurted out.

"Go on, then."

But as Martin rose shakily to his feet, Captain Kinlata walked into the stuffy little cabin.

"And how do you find him?" he asked.

"He's obviously got a fever." Martin didn't really know what to say; he was still too shocked.

"We'll take care of him," said the captain, and Ali closed his eyes as if to blot out everything around him. "Now—" Captain Kinlata's voice became commanding—"I must ask you to leave. The storm's coming nearer."

"But what will *you* do?" insisted Martin. "Suppose the ship starts breaking up?"

Captain Kinlata smiled. "It's good of you to be concerned. But I gather from the coast guard and the weather stations that the storm may not be strong enough for that."

"But you can't tell—"

"If anything goes wrong, I am assured the residents of Shetland are standing by us, and so are the rescue services. I am so very grateful and so are the ship's owners. Now—you must go."

"Bye, Ali," Martin said gently.

But Ali didn't open his eyes and, as they left, Martin felt leaden and hopeless. If Eric was right, could he have been deceiving himself, jumping to conclusions? Supposing Eric was lying? But then, why should he? And Ali—why was he so afraid?

"Good-bye, and don't worry. We shall be safe." Captain Kinlata stood at the top of the gangway as they hurried down.

When they were out of earshot, Martin snapped, "The car *must* have been there."

"And I tell you it wasn't," said Eric equally firmly.

"I suppose you think I made it all up?"

"No—no, I don't. They could have moved it," he added doubtfully.

They walked on. Suddenly, Martin stopped dead.

"Now what?" asked Eric impatiently.

"You left the knife in your saddlebag."

Eric's eyes widened. "Oh, my God! How could I have been so—" He broke off and ran around to the back of one of the roofless crofts, where they had put the bikes, and rummaged in the saddlebag. Seconds later he let out a howl of rage. "It's gone!" he yelled. "The knife's gone!"

"What's up, son?"

Martin wheeled around. Strolling out of one of the crofts was Magnus Dunglas. Beside him stood his tall, wiry son, Peter. His face, like Eric's, was a mess, and his fists, hanging by his sides, were clasped tight.

Martin felt completely trapped and the gradually nearing claps of thunder served only to make the situation more menacing. There seemed to be a strange, unfamiliar light in Magnus's eyes; they looked almost excited, confident of victory.

Eric was clearly unafraid; his anger was far too great for that—his anger and his sense of loss. "Where is it?" he rapped.

Peter gave him a mocking smile. "Where's what?"

"You know what I mean."

"Do I?" He laughed, and Eric advanced on him.

"You want to carry on where we left off?"

"Why not?"

But before they could spring at each other, Magnus and his vast bulk was between them. "I don't know what's biting you two, but you can finish demolishing each other at school. Not in front of me."

Eric hesitated and then shrugged. But his anger was still there, smoldering away. "He's got something of mine."

"What can that be?" asked Magnus gently.

"Something precious."

"I haven't taken anything, Dad," protested Peter.

"It was in my saddlebag."

"*What* was in your saddlebag?" asked Magnus impatiently.

"I'm not saying," said Eric stubbornly.

"Then how do we know what we're talking about?" said Magnus with heavy reasonableness. "Come *on*, son."

"*He* knows," yelled Eric.

"We're getting nowhere."

"I want him *searched*."

"Turn out your pockets, Peter. Anything to satisfy him," Magnus grunted.

Have they got it? Martin wondered. It was impossible to tell.

Slowly, mockingly, Peter turned out his pockets while, with utmost gravity, Magnus did the same. It was clear they didn't have the knife on them.

"You've hidden it somewhere," Eric accused. He

looked vaguely around him, conscious of the gathering absurdity of his position.

Martin, meanwhile, didn't know what to do. He looked up at the mauve-black swollen storm clouds, heard the grumble of the thunder, and shuddered. Suddenly, a flash of blue lightning lit up the four of them and again Martin stared straight into Magnus's eyes. This time they seemed blank, expressionless, not in the least villainous.

"You'd better search the place," said Magnus. "We have other things to think about. Don't you realize the danger the *Saturn*'s in? I'm bringing back some of the lads; we're going to back up the rescue services if they're needed. We may have to help get men off that ship fast. Come on, Peter."

They walked hurriedly away without a backward glance, leaving Martin to wonder what Eric's next move would be.

"I'm going to search these crofts," said Eric. "They may have stashed it away there."

"You're really sure they took it?" asked Martin. Eric's conviction that there was a tractor under the tarpaulin had undermined his confidence in the whole situation.

Eric turned on Martin and sneered as more thunder growled. "You don't know our families, do you? Our history."

"I know Magnus—"

"You know what he seems to be," said Eric quietly. "It's like Dad—they're of the old island—the Norse people."

"But I don't see—"

"They want things to be the way they were, but they can't be like that again." Eric spoke with great conviction. "They want Shetland to be a real crofting community again; that's the one thing they have in common. It's an obsession, a kind of justification for their lives." He paused. "I think they're pathetic."

"But why?"

"Times have changed, the world has progressed. They're trying to turn the clock back."

"But why are they against each other? They've got a lot in common, haven't they?" pursued Martin.

Eric suddenly looked as if he'd said too much. "They go about things in different ways," he muttered. "Dad's such a purist and Magnus . . ."

"Yes?"

"He's an animal. Like his son."

Martin was completely mystified. What kind of rivalries had he stumbled into?

"Do you want me to help you look?"

"No. Go back home. Your parents will be worried with the storm coming on."

"But I want to—"

"No. They'll only blame me. We could be friends. Do a bit of fishing sometime. It doesn't matter that I'm older. Does it?" he asked challengingly.

"It doesn't matter," replied Martin gratefully.

"Then go. I must search. After that I'll just wait here and watch what happens to the boat in the storm."

"What about Peter?"

"Oh, him. I'll straighten him out. When I've got the knife back."

But suppose you don't find it, wondered Martin. What then?

Martin rode hard out of Settler, up the hill and toward home. It was only when he had been riding for about five minutes that he detected a rattling in his saddlebag. Vaguely he wondered what was making the noise. Had his tool kit come apart? He stopped on the brow of the hill, leaned his bike against a rock, and walked around to his saddlebag. As he did so, Martin heard a rustling sound from somewhere higher up the hillside. He paused and then continued. It was probably a fox or something. Opening the bag, he felt inside. The storm had made everything prematurely dark, and it was difficult to see, but when he made contact with the object, Martin froze. He knew all too well what was in his saddlebag. It was the silver-bladed knife.

Martin's whole body went rigid, and then he began to shake so hard that he had to lean against the rock. Someone had put it in there. It must have been Magnus or his son. Who else? Why? Whatever the reason, they were bound to rob him on the way home. He was sure of it. He heard the rustling again and looked at his bike. He had to get on it fast. Now. And pedal really fast. But what if they had a vehicle? Did they have one? He was so confused he couldn't remember. Either way, they would be after him, ready to grab the knife. So should he stay here? Were they somewhere on the hill? Waiting at the bottom?

Martin grabbed his bike and was just about to mount it when something landed on his shoulders, and he and the bike parted company.

Six

Martin fell onto the uneven surface of the road with a weight pressing him down. He tried to roll over, but the weight was too great and his face was pressed down onto the broken tarmac. Then, with surprising agility, his attacker released him, and as Martin turned painfully onto his back, he saw a slim figure, dressed in black, rooting through his saddle-bag. In a second he had grabbed the knife. Martin didn't stop to think; every instinct told him he wasn't going to let the knife go again that easily. He flung himself at his attacker's legs, and when Martin brought him down, the knife clattered to the ground. As they rolled over, Martin gave a cry of horror. His opponent had been wearing a cat mask, but in the struggle it came off, revealing a familiar face. It was Ali.

"It's you."

Ali didn't reply. He pushed Martin away from him

and stood up. His eyes looked wild and disoriented and he was sweating profusely. Ali dived for the knife again, and Martin dived with him. They rolled over and over, struggling to reach the knife.

"I'm sorry," said Ali at length, and brought his fist crashing into Martin's face.

When he came to, Martin was in the back of a van being driven at relentless speed toward the sea. His head ached horribly and he felt vaguely sick. Ali—his face came into Martin's mind, and with it an image of the cat mask he had been wearing. Obviously he had wanted to conceal his identity. But why was Ali involved? Why was *he* after the knife? The complications seemed endless. The van continued to pitch and toss and then, quite suddenly, the vehicle stopped and the back door was flung open.

"Get out," said Ali.

Martin struggled out, his head spinning. He didn't feel capable of fighting anymore. He just wanted to sit down somewhere and hold his head in his hands.

"Now, don't try anything."

Martin shook his head hopelessly and stared muzzily around him. He was outside an old van, near the sea, in a small cove that he remembered exploring when they had first moved to Shetland. It was the next one to Settler. The sea was making a hollow booming sound and the thunder was loud overhead. Jagged flashes of lightning lit up the sky while the moon rode overhead, looking too full, too white to be healthy. The waves were enormous, rushing up the beach in a cloud of demonic spray.

"I thought you were ill," Martin accused Ali warily.

"I am," Ali replied shakily but with conviction. He's right, thought Martin, he looks terrible.

"Then what are you doing out here? Who does this van belong to?"

"They made me come. I had to get the knife."

"Who put it in my saddlebag?"

"I can't tell you that."

"It must have been Magnus—or Peter."

"I don't want to talk about it." The beads of perspiration on Ali's forehead were now running into his eyes.

"Who are *they*?" persisted Martin, his head clearing a little. "Who are they to make you do all this—dress up in that silly costume, come out here in this weather when you're so ill? And what about us? I thought we were going to be friends." Somehow, in the midst of everything, this was what upset Martin most.

"I told you, I don't want to talk about it. We have to get in the boat." Ali sounded desperate.

"What boat?" Then he saw it—a small rubber dinghy drawn up on the shore above the tide line. A new fear seized him. "We're not going to sea?"

Ali nodded. "I remembered the dinghy was here." There was a note of pride in his voice.

"We'll drown."

"No."

"It's too rough!"

"I've been on lakes in a high wind. We'll be fine." But he didn't sound very confident.

"I'm not budging."

"I'll have to hurt you again."

"Try it," said Martin unsteadily.

"I'm stronger than you are. Please trust me," said Ali with sudden gentleness. "You must cooperate. You can't stay here. It's not safe for you."

"Where are we going?" Martin stared at the boiling sea in abject fear. They would drown, both of them. Ali must be crazy—he certainly looked it.

"We're going to the *Saturn*."

"Why in a boat? We can walk around." He *was* crazy.

"There will be people on the beach. They would see us."

"Why are you kidnapping me like this?" said Martin, staring at Ali in anguish.

"You *must* come with me. You're not safe alone.

On the *Saturn* I can take care of you."

"The *Saturn* may be breaking up."

"No, it'll be all right. We've been in worse storms." Ali sounded very sure.

"Not sitting on the rocks," Martin reminded him.

"It'll be *okay*, I tell you." There was a distinct edge to his voice now.

"Why can't we go by land?" he persisted.

Ali stepped closer to him. "Stop talking, Martin."

"Why can't we go by land?" he repeated stubbornly.

"I told you—because we'll be seen."

"We'll be seen anyway."

"We'll be coming up on her other side."

"We'll capsize."

"Stop arguing and help push out the dinghy. I'm doing it all for *you*."

"Ali—"

"Come *on*."

Miserable, Martin did as he was told. Together they pushed the frail-looking craft into the lashing waves.

"Get in."

Without any further procrastination, Martin jumped in, quickly followed by Ali, as the rubber dinghy tore through the foam and then began to bounce wildly over the crests.

It was much worse than even Martin had imagined. One moment the dinghy was wallowing in the troughs, the next it was shuddering up over huge waves and down the other side. Every second Martin thought they would capsize, but somehow they survived as Ali rowed grimly around the point. The rocks on the shore were dark and primeval, and now that night had fallen, they reared out of the tumult of water, needle-sharp and hugely menacing. The wind howled among them and the spray was a deathly white.

With the knife jammed provocatively into his belt, Ali rowed very strongly and the dinghy began to make real progress despite the unrestrained violence of the elements. Once they were farther out to sea, the wind seemed to quiet, and although the waves were still enormous, there was an increasingly sinister stillness.

Ali passed Martin a plastic box. "Bail," he said, rowing on with fiercely athletic determination.

As Martin dutifully bailed water over the side, the wind suddenly sank to almost nothing. "Is it over?" he asked fearfully.

"No."

"What then?"

"It's the eye of the storm. The still part. It'll come back soon."

It was very eerie, with the sky a black hollow and the sea rolling on below. The moon was obscured now, and there was no sign of any stars.

"What's going to happen when we get to the *Saturn*?"

"You're going to have to be kept out of sight."

"For how long?" Martin asked anxiously.

"A few hours."

"And then?"

"We'll let you go. We'll be off limits by then."

"The *Saturn* won't be able to sail."

"Forget the *Saturn*. We're going on another ship."

"All of you?" Martin didn't know whether to believe him or not.

"Yes."

"But there aren't any other African ships—" He broke off as Ali grinned.

"We don't need one—we're going on a Polish klondyker. Then we'll transfer."

"I know you've got the antiques. You'll transfer them too, I suppose."

"All the gold and silver stuff. Yes."

"Is it worth a lot?"

"A fortune."

"My parents—" began Martin.

"We'll phone them. Say you're safe."

"Will you *really* let me go?" He could still hardly believe what was happening. But the eye of the storm had calmed him as well as the waves, although he was terrified of it all starting again. The sky was a horrible mauve color, and it looked decidedly unpredictable.

"Soon as we put to sea. We'll leave you."

"You mean, I'll be on my own on the *Saturn*?" Martin was appalled, his momentary calmness shattered.

"You'll be safe. I promise. We'll let them know where you are. You won't be alone for long. And just remember to keep your mouth shut. You'll be okay if you keep quiet about all this."

"Why are you mixed up in it?" Martin asked hesitantly.

"I want to make some money," said Ali simply.

"Money—you're doing all this, treating me like this—just for the money?" There was deep hurt in Martin's voice.

"My parents are poor farmers. So are my brothers and sisters. You don't understand—I *must* help them. And I will," he finished determinedly.

"So it's Magnus and Peter—they organized all this."

"I can't say," he repeated. "Keep bailing."

"It is them, isn't it?"

"Just shut up," yelled Ali.

Thunder growled from somewhere far off.

"Is it starting again?" asked Martin, instantly worried about the weather.

"Feels like it."

But they were around the rocks now and could see the dim shape of the stern of the *Saturn*.

"Don't shout out," Ali threatened.

"What if I do?"

"I'll pitch you out; you won't stand a chance in this sea." He laughed uncertainly. Martin was pretty sure he wouldn't actually do it, but he definitely didn't want to put Ali to the test.

"What now, then?"

"They're waiting. Look."

A group of men was huddled around the stern. Two rope ladders were draped over the side, but waves were already pounding against them.

"We're going up there?"

"Sure."

"I won't make it."

"You'll have to" came the crisp reply, almost drowned in a clap of thunder. "I'll bring the dinghy around, then jump for the ladder."

"I can't."

"Get ready."

"No!"

"Now."

But Martin remained where he was, and the dinghy turned away from the stern of the *Saturn*.

"I'm coming around again."

"I'm not jumping," Martin pleaded.

"You damn well are. I'm going in again."

"No."

"Now—jump."

This time Martin jumped.

He managed to grab the wet rope of the ladder and hang on despite the fact that he was continually submerged in mountainous waves.

"Climb," said a voice at the top.

But he couldn't; all he could do was hang on, pressing himself into the ladder, gasping as each successive wave hit him. Then he felt strong arms behind him and, looking down, saw that Ali had lashed the dinghy to the other rope ladder and was now hanging on, almost straddling him. "Climb," he said. "Climb or I'll fall."

Slowly, haltingly, Martin began to climb upward until he was clear of Ali. Still the water pounded at him, but still he climbed.

Struggling and gasping, Martin was quickly

pulled over onto the stern deck of the *Saturn* which was continually being submerged in the waves. Ali was behind him as Martin was half dragged, half carried by a group of men toward the rusting super-structure, and finally into the dark dryness of a companionway which was lit by a pale bulb.

"Are you okay?" Ali asked breathlessly.

"I'm okay."

The men around Martin looked relieved, exchanging anxious glances. "We were worried about you, Ali," said one of them. "Skipper's gone ashore looking for you."

"Had to rescue the boy," said Ali, and before anyone could question him further, he pushed Martin down to his cabin.

"Let me go," pleaded Martin as Ali dragged him to the bunk. The pounding of tons of water outside and the continuous vibration of the *Saturn* terrified him. But Ali shook his head.

"You won't be here long. Put these things on and try to get some sleep."

"No chance," retorted Martin.

"If you promise to keep quiet, I'll get a message to your parents. Tell them you'll be back in the morning. They won't be able to search for you tonight. Not in this weather."

"I suppose 'they'll' tell them," said Martin bitterly. "Whoever 'they' are."

Ali didn't reply.

Ali returned quite quickly with a mug of steaming hot chocolate. Martin was lying in the bunk wearing Ali's track suit, his wet clothes discarded on the floor.

"I've told them you're staying with friends," he said, passing Martin the chocolate and starting to take off his own soaking clothes.

"They won't believe that—I don't have any friends," said Martin, and was immediately annoyed with himself for sounding so self-pitying.

Ali took no notice. "Drink your hot chocolate" was all he said, rubbing himself down vigorously.

With a display of reluctance Martin put the cup to his lips. It was absolutely delicious.

"Why did you bring me here? Why—"

"I couldn't leave you there," Ali cut in unexpectedly. "Not in this weather. You could have died of exposure if I'd knocked you unconscious again and you'd have been out there till morning. And I was afraid for you. You've found out too much. . . ." His voice trailed away.

Martin took another sip of the excellent hot chocolate, feeling a sudden surge of happiness. Ali did like him after all. He'd risked a lot to help him. Warmth began to spread through him and his eyes started to close. Ali's face was receding into a blur, and the tiny cabin filled with a crashing blackness.

The blankets were heaving like a wild night at sea and Martin felt that he was back in the storm-tossed dinghy. A steady, shrilling wind blew hard in his face, and once again he was soaked through. He opened his eyes and saw above him a ragged sky torn by hurtling clouds with a cold, sodden orb mistily showing through. It was some time before he realized it was the sun. He knew he was dreaming. But he was so dreadfully cold. Where were the sheets, the blankets? And he had a pounding headache.

"Stay where you are."

The boat seemed to shoot up one wave and down the other.

"Stay where you are." The command was repeated abruptly.

He opened his eyes again to see Ali rowing in the bow. They were in a rubber dinghy, but a much bigger one this time, and on the floor between them was a pile of boxes.

"You're moving around," said Ali. "Don't."

Was it a dream? No—it was too wet and cold and his head hurt too much.

"Where are we going?" he muttered.

"Filla."

"The island?"

"There aren't two."

"What's happened?" He struggled to sit upright, his headache vibrating horribly.

"It broke up."

"No!"

"We never thought it would. But it broke in two." Ali's voice trembled.

"Is everyone all right?"

"They got off; the storm's easier now. The group on the beach rigged up a line. But somehow I managed to lower this dinghy from the stern. And you—and all this." He indicated the boxes. "Shows what you can do if you're desperate," he said, and there was a sudden note of bitterness in his voice.

"I suppose the Hoard's in those boxes?" said Martin, his head feeling as if it were splitting.

"The antiques—yes."

Martin closed his eyes. It was like a nightmare to be back on the sea again, and he felt a crushing sense of his own helplessness. He began to shiver and Ali looked at him anxiously.

"I'm really sorry," he said.

"What about my parents? My sister? You just want to get the money, don't you?"

"For my family. They could die." The sincerity and passion shone so hard out of Ali's eyes that for a moment Martin felt overwhelmed. Then, as a particularly large wave broke over the boat, he was jerked back into the present situation.

"So could I," he muttered.

"I *am* sorry. Very sorry." Ali rowed ever harder, putting everything he could into his battle with the sea. Filla was on the horizon and the sea was gradually getting calmer, although running a tremendous swell. "We'll try the outboard now," said Ali. "It was too rough before."

He crossed the dinghy slowly and Martin could see that he still looked feverish and his face was more gray than brown.

"You're worse, aren't you?"

"I'll be all right."

"Like you said the *Saturn* would be all right."

"Shut up!" he shouted, but Martin could see that his hands were shaking.

The outboard started immediately and they began to make more progress toward Filla.

"When will we get there?"

" 'Bout an hour."

"Then what?"

"We'll hide the antiques."

"The Hoard," Martin corrected him.

"Whatever," said Ali indifferently. "And then I'll get you back."

"Will you be in time for the Polish klondyker?"

"Yes," he said fiercely. "I have to be. And I have to be paid."

"By who?"

"I'm not saying."

"Not even now?"

"Not even now."

"You drugged that hot chocolate," said Martin angrily, "and I've got a headache." Suddenly he felt like bursting into tears. "A bad headache." He looked at Ali, who was now shivering violently. "You *are* worse—you're really sick."

"I'll be fine," Ali replied doggedly.

This seemed to be the last straw to Martin. Filla was uninhabited, cold, and wild and inhospitable. Suppose Ali passed out on him? What on earth was he going to do?

After another half hour the sea began to flatten out and the wind to drop. Martin was feeling better, although he was desperately worried about his parents and about Ali, who was now noticeably worse: The sweating and shivering seemed more pronounced and his hands were trembling. Filla was bigger now, its forbidding rocks lashed by the sea, calmer though it was. There seemed no way of landing, but maybe Ali knew of somewhere around the other side. He could see gulls and other seabirds perched on the jagged rocks, and he caught a glimpse of what he thought was a colony of seals riding the breakers just offshore.

But when Martin looked at Ali again, he saw that his head had dropped to his chest and his hand was only very loosely on the tiller. Soon the dinghy began to weave around.

"Ali?"

There was no response.

"Ali."

"Mmm?"

"Ali. You're dropping off to sleep."

"Mmm."

"The dinghy's out of control."

"Mmm." Ali's hand gradually began to slip off the tiller.

Martin sat horror-struck. They were bearing down on the island with its vicious rocks and barren interior. There was not a tree, hardly a tuft of grass—just rock and more rock, hard and unyielding. Every second took the dinghy nearer to the grim foreshore, which under the lowering gray sky looked like the gateway to hell.

"How do we get in?"

Ali said nothing, just slumped there without even a grunt this time. His hand had slipped right off the tiller and the dinghy was now circling. With only limited experience of boats, it was still quite evident to Martin that they were in great danger; a gray swell was running toward the island, and every time the dinghy came up against it, it pitched and tossed, and Martin guessed it wouldn't be long before they were broached to and overturned. They would stand no chance in the sea, he thought, and as for the Hoard—it would lie at the bottom of the ocean forever. Maybe that's the best place for it, thought Martin fleetingly.

He must do something—take over the tiller and search for a landing space—and he must do it now. With sudden decision Martin struggled stiffly and awkwardly to his feet and plunged across the boat toward Ali. Immediately the dinghy tipped up and the Hoard slid toward him. Hurriedly, Martin moved back, righting the dinghy again while Ali still remained slumped across the tiller. What could he do? The swell was driving them onto the rocks, and if he couldn't shift Ali, they would capsize.

"Listen, Ali."

No response.

"For God's sake—listen."

"Mmm."

Well, at least he was back to grunting again. Martin gave a shout of alarm as the dinghy rose on the swell and almost stood on end. The boxes shifted toward Ali, but somehow Martin managed to cling onto his position and, miraculously, the dinghy righted itself.

"Ali—we're going to capsize. You have to listen."

"Mmm."

"Ali!"

He opened his eyes a fraction.

"Ali."

"Yes?"

"You're ill. You've got to change places with me."

"I can't."

"If you don't, we'll capsize. We must cross over before we circle around again."

"Okay."

"Do it now."

But he remained slumped there, immobile.

"Do it now."

Still he lay there.

"Do it *now*!" screamed Martin. "Do it *now*."

With a terrible determination Ali struggled to his feet and plunged across the dinghy. At the same time, Martin did the same, grabbing the tiller and straightening the fragile, bobbing craft.

Slowly the boat came around and began to head toward the impenetrable fortress of Filla's rocks.

"Don't go back to sleep, Ali, Wake up!"

"What?"

"Where are we going? Where's a harbor?"

"Can't remember exactly."

"So what do we do?"

"Cove around the other side maybe. Stay out. Watch the rocks. If the boat catches one, it'll tear us apart."

Martin could see that Ali was making the most incredible effort to speak.

"Okay. I keep out. Where do I go?"

"Right out. Farther out. Go around Filla." Ali's head slumped to his chest again, and Martin knew that he was on his own.

Seven

It seemed to take hours to beat his way through the choppy seas that protected Filla, and because of his total lack of experience the voyage terrified Martin more and more.

Gradually the dinghy swung around the island, bobbing alarmingly in the swell and making slow progress around the headland. Ali was slumped in the prow of the dinghy, and although Martin spoke to him several times, he made no reply. What was worse, his breathing had become deeper and much slower. But Martin knew that all he could do, for the moment, was to concentrate on finding a spot for a safe landing. He had never imagined the sea to be as strong and as violent a force as this—but on the other hand, he had never imagined himself on it. The Shetland sea was cold and greeny dark— treacherous in its wildness. As the dinghy breasted another wave, Martin had a fleeting mental glimpse of a Mediterranean beach where he had once gone on vacation. The burning sun, the drone of the sun worshippers, the licking waves on the sandy foreshore—the image vanished as he saw boiling foam lash the deadly rocks, which seemed even higher and more impenetrable as the other side of Filla came into view. Here the sea was short and choppy, but at least he was out of the rolling swell that had always threatened to capsize them.

Then Martin saw what he thought was some kind of mirage—a minute cove with a gravelly beach. But there was a barrage of rocks in the way—some looming out of the sea like accusing fingers, others half buried, noticeable only by the breaking surf. Could he steer the dinghy through? He'd have to.

Slowly, gingerly, his nerves taut with fear, Martin managed to get a little closer to the cove, throttling back the outboard by instinct. But the choppy sea made the dinghy bounce horrendously, and as soon as it was among the half-submerged rocks, Martin felt the cold grip of panic. To help himself, to steady his hands, to stop himself screaming, Martin began a trembling commentary to himself, spoken out loud in relentless machine-gun delivery: "Right a bit and now straight and now on and a bit left and a bit right and a bit more right and on and on . . ."

Several times the outboard motor caught a projection but wrenched itself away. At other moments the waves sent the dinghy careering over smooth, foamy humpbacks of rocks, just avoiding jagged edges and ridged shelves. But Martin knew his luck wouldn't hold forever, and when he was only yards from the beach he heard the ripping of the dinghy's underside as it was pushed sideways over a needle-sharp rock. It came clear abruptly, but with water spouting from the numerous holes.

"We're sinking," yelled Martin, but Ali didn't reply, his breathing heavier, more labored. In desperation Martin put the outboard on full throttle, and the dinghy raced through the foamy green breakers like a surfboard until, with a shuddering thump, it hit the beach, half full of water and now with a great rent in its bottom.

Stiff-legged, Martin jumped out and, using all his waning strength, he dragged the rubber dinghy up the beach. The outboard kept getting caught, and several times Ali almost slipped out into the pounding surf.

Ten minutes later Martin had dragged it beyond the waves. Ali and the Hoard were safe and he was utterly exhausted. But his ordeal was not over yet. Ali lay half in and half out of the dinghy. He was up to his waist in water and his breathing now was more like snorting.

He's going to die, thought Martin frantically as he put his hands under Ali's arms and started to pull. He's going to die. The phrase repeated itself relentlessly in Martin's mind.

Eventually Martin managed to drag Ali out of the dinghy and up the beach until he was lying on the pebbles, his limbs splayed and his eyes closed. I've got to light a fire, Martin thought. Somehow I've got to light a fire. But what with?

Martin began to search for shelter, but there was nothing except a shallow indentation—it could scarcely be called a cave—in the cliff. With his last shred of energy Martin pulled Ali against this inlet, propped him up, and looked around for something to cover him with. Ali's stentorian, hoarse breathing seemed to be getting worse every moment, but there was absolutely nothing in sight for protection—only rock and pebble. Martin knew he would have to climb up into the heart of the island and see what he could find. But he was not optimistic, for he was sure that Filla was only a clump of barren rock and that his chances of saving Ali's life were slim indeed.

A renewed tide of panic overcame Martin as he scrambled up the sloping rocky cliff. He was wet and shivering when he started, but the steep scramble warmed him, and when he finally stood up and surveyed the interior he was sweating slightly and his clothes were sticking damply to him.

At first sight the island was all he had expected: bare rock, peat, wiry tussocky grass and a few stunted clumps of heather. Then he saw that on the far side there was a small stone building huddled against a steeply rising promontory.

Running to keep warm, he stumbled across the uneven ground, birds wheeling up around him with keening calls. The island had a feeling of very great age, of holding secrets firmly clasped to its ancient rocky bosom. He passed piles of weathered stone, the remains of some ancient settlement. Then he was at the building and suddenly his hopes soared. It was intact, well built, with a new roof and a small notice saying FILLA ORNITHOLOGICAL CLUB.

He had stumbled on a bird-watching center, but when he tried the heavy wooden door, it remained firmly locked. Searching around on the ground, he lifted several large stones and eventually found a key. Inserting it in the lock, he twisted it and the door rattled open. But then he could have wept with disappointment. Inside was what looked like a completely bare room.

Martin gloomily surveyed the empty space. The door banged closed behind him and, turning around sharply, he gave a shout of joy. Behind the door was a cupboard that contained a pack of matches, a kettle, blankets, a portable stove, some cans of food, pots, plates, cutlery, and a lamp with a bottle of kerosene. Another notice read: PLEASE REPLACE EMERGENCY STOCKS WHEN USED.

Martin paused, trying to think the situation out logically while a newly rising wind howled and clamored around the island. There was no way he could bring Ali up, so he would have to take the supplies down to him. The blankets first and the matches, so that he could try to light a fire. Food later. And what about water? Maybe there was a spring somewhere. Surely the kettle wasn't there just to mock him, or did the bird watchers bring their own water with them in containers? Either way, the immediate priority for Ali was blankets and matches. Putting a box of matches in his pocket, Martin staggered out with as many blankets as he could carry.

When Martin eventually clambered back down the rocks to the cove, he was surprised to find Ali's breathing a little quieter and more regular. Working fast, he took off Ali's wet clothes— a difficult and

cumbersome process—and then with equal difficulty he wrapped him in layer after layer of blanket.
By the time he had finished, the sun was riding high
in the sky, and when he looked at his watch, it was
nine-thirty. Almost numb with exhaustion now, his
body screaming for rest, he just wanted to lie down
and sleep forever. But he knew he had to keep going.

There wasn't much driftwood around, but after
half an hour Martin had gathered enough for at least
the basis of a fire. He remembered his brief period in
the cub scouts, the forced jollity of the leaders having finally driven him to quit. But at least he had
been taught how to light a fire, so he built his small
stack of kindling into a wigwam shape, added bigger
sticks and brush, and tried to set it alight. For a frus-
trating twenty minutes nothing happened; it was
just too damp. Then a tiny spark caught and then
another, until there was a center cone of fragile
flame. Martin nursed the flickering pale warmth,
growing elated as it glowed harder and became real
heat. Then the fire started crackling greedily and he
began to worry about the limited pile of fuel he had
gathered.

Martin spent the next hour rushing around
searching for more driftwood, and after much lug-
ging he had a reasonable stock. The fire blazed

higher and he dragged Ali over to lie beside the delicious spreading warmth.

Martin sat staring into the flames, knowing that sooner or later he must climb up again to bring down some food from the stone house—and to search for some drinking water. But he felt too shattered to do so immediately, and the more he stared into the flames, the more sleep overtook him. Gradually Martin's head sunk down, and he involuntarily stretched out in luxurious relaxation. He was warm, still, drifting. Martin slept. He dreamed of the Mediterranean beach again, playing ball with his mother while his father swam in the sea with Clare. An old man was selling coconuts and a big white yacht was sailing listlessly on the horizon.

"Martin."

Someone was swimming lazily toward them, his black face grinning up from the water.

"Martin."

The face was calling his name, but he went on playing ball.

"Martin."

At last the voice penetrated and he opened his eyes reluctantly to see the flickering flames and the breaking gray sea beyond.

Ali was half sitting up, wheezing, and with sweat

pouring down his face again.

"How you feeling?" Martin dragged himself over to him.

"Bad."

"Stay in those blankets."

"Where's the Hoard?"

"Safe in the dinghy."

Ali seemed to relax a little until he was disturbed again by a dry racking cough.

"They'll come to get us."

"Who?"

"They'll come." He lay back and closed his eyes. Ali's voice grew fainter. "They'll come. We must hide."

Martin wondered who Ali was so afraid of. Surely they would be fools to try and hide; they desperately needed a rescue, from absolutely anyone.

Slowly and painfully, Martin clambered up the cliff again and made his way to the stone house. He could see the sea on three sides, and there was no sign of any craft at all. But he wanted to make absolutely certain, so he scrambled up the promontory and looked over the remaining seascape. Apart from a tanker right out on the horizon, there was nothing, so he climbed down, collected cans, an opener, a pot, cutlery, the stove, and the kettle and stuffed them into a battered old shopping bag he found at the bottom of the cupboard. Then he began the descent to the beach. He would search for water later.

When Martin returned, Ali was asleep and his breathing, although still rasping, was again more regular, less labored. He lit the stove and a small blue flame spluttered into life. Then he opened a can of beans and frankfurters, put them in the old pot, and began to heat them. The smell was incredibly appetizing, and for the first time Martin realized how hungry he was.

He shook Ali awake and, getting out a filthy, damp handkerchief, he gently began to wipe away the sweat on Ali's forehead. But it was no good—the cold beads of moisture just reappeared.

"What's matter?" Ali asked blearily.

"I'm cooking."

"What?"

"I'm making food."

"Not hungry."

"You've *got* to eat," Martin insisted.

"Want to sleep."

"*Eat.*"

"Not hungry."

"Try this." Martin grabbed a rusty tin spoon, dipped it into the baked beans, and tried to feed him. But he spat them out.

"Want to sleep."

"You *can't*."

"Why not?"

"You'll die."

"Die?" Ali sounded very surprised, and his eyes opened just a little wider. "Die?"

"You've got a fever, and now you're probably suffering from exposure. You've got to eat. You *must* try."

Ali managed to swallow a few spoonfuls but then he sank back. "Enough."

"More."

"No."

But he did manage another mouthful before he slumped back. This must be what feeding a baby's like, thought Martin. A very reluctant baby.

After he had finished eating, Martin built up the fire until it was a strong, warm glow and curled up beside it, promising himself that he would doze for only a few minutes. But almost at once he fell into a deep, dreamless sleep. When he woke, it was because someone was tugging at his shoulder.

"Go away, Ali."

"Come on."

"Go away." Martin slowly opened his eyes. He was looking up into the face of Eric, and standing behind him was Dr. West.

"You okay?" asked Eric.

"Sure."

"And Ali?"

"He's bad."

"Let *me* look," said Dr. West. "I'm an archaeologist, not a medical doctor, but I do know a bit about first aid." He smiled reassuringly, and Martin felt a wave of relief. By some miracle, help had come. Maybe another hour or so and Ali would have been dead, or they would both have been dead. But now they were saved. It was almost too amazing to be true. Then he glanced up again at Eric, and he suddenly felt uneasy. There was something horribly wrong. But what could it be?

"How did you know we were here?" asked Martin.

"Put two and two together," said Dr. West in his reassuring, professional way.

Eric walked slowly over to the dinghy. "It's all here, Dad."

Something stirred in Martin's stomach—a flutter, like a moth around a light—but at the moment his main concern was Ali. "How's Ali?" he asked anxiously. "Will he be all right?"

"He's got a nasty fever and it's gone to his chest. But he'll live."

"Thank goodness."

"He brought you out here?" Dr. West asked quite sharply.

"Yes—with the antiques."

"Trying to steal them, was he?"

"I don't know exactly. He said something about hiding them. But I do know he expected money from someone—for his family, he said."

"This was no way to help them." Dr. West's voice was stern. Eric stood by the dinghy. There's something odd about Dr. West, thought Martin. He looks different somehow. But he couldn't put his finger on it.

"He also said something about a Polish klondyker. He had to meet it."

"The *Poznań*?"

"I don't know."

"Well, he's not going to now, is he?" Dr. West laughed, and suddenly Martin sensed that the reassurance had gone out of his voice. Instead, there was a carelessness to him, and when Martin looked at Eric, he could see that he was afraid.

Dr. West started to say something else, but Ali's eyes were open now and he was staring at him. Then Ali whispered huskily, "Can I have my money now?"

Dr. West laughed again. It was a very unpleasant sound and Martin felt utterly confused. What on earth was going on? Why was Ali asking Dr. West for money? The moth in his stomach fluttered again and became bigger, more insistent.

"Money?" said Dr. West. "You'll be lucky to get out of here alive." He chuckled.

"Dad," began Eric. "We've got to help him. Now."

"It doesn't matter whether he lives or dies, does it?" The cruel note in Dr. West's voice was more pronounced, and Eric turned away, looking out to sea, his hands in his pockets. But his shoulders were rigid with tension.

"What do you mean?" demanded Martin.

"You do understand the contents of those boxes aren't *just* antiques, don't you?" said Dr. West slowly.

"They said—they said they were made from the Hoard," muttered Martin. "But it's all some silly old legend anyway."

"And who is 'they'?"

"Magnus."

"And he claims to own the Hoard, does he?" Dr. West came over and stood very close to Martin.

"No—no, of course not." Martin's voice trembled

as he began to realize how strangely Eric's father was behaving. What on earth was the matter with him, he wondered. Why was he acting like this? There was something obsessive about him, something horribly uncaring.

Dr. West spoke sharply, angrily. "It's ours," he said.

"Yours?"

"We're the oldest family. The Settler family."

"I don't understand."

"The Hoard is ours; it belonged to our ancestors." Dr. West stood up, a dark shadow against the sun. His eyes glittered and there was a madness in them that made Martin more afraid than he'd ever been of the sea. "We have deeds to prove we lived in Settler—that the Hoard was handed into our safe-keeping. I took good care of it in the museum, but it was mine really."

"Magnus stole it," Eric broke in quickly, his back still turned to Martin. "He hid it in that croft at Settler; it disappeared for years until I found it."

"So the knife is part of the Hoard," said Martin.

"It wasn't easy to move it," said Eric, ignoring him. He turned around, his eyes wide with fear. "Not with the local kids wondering where I was going."

"So you wore the cat mask." Martin spoke flatly. "And it was you who knocked me down that first time."

"Yes . . ." Eric looked across at him sadly.

"And it was *you* who put the knife in my saddle-bag," Martin accused him.

"No—no. That was Magnus," he said, and looked directly at Martin for the first time.

"And he sent Ali to take it back?" Martin sounded very skeptical.

Eric nodded.

"Magnus knew his hiding place had been discovered," said Dr. West, his voice expressionless now, "so they bided their time until we got it together at my cottage."

Eric flashed his father a warning glance, and Martin suddenly lost his temper.

"They didn't steal it in the first place, did they?" he yelled. "You're making it all up. Both of you. It was you who stole it from the museum, Dr. West. It was you who stashed the Hoard away in Settler—you who got the captain of the *Saturn* to smuggle it out. You could hardly use anyone from the islands or do it yourself. It'd soon leak out. But an African klondyker—that was really clever." Martin paused for breath. "Ali was just an errand boy, wasn't he?"

he said bitterly. "Yet you promised him a fortune. And there must have been more of the Hoard stashed away in the Lada—I know that car's on the *Saturn* somewhere."

Dr. West smiled his glittering smile. "I assure you there can be nothing left in the car now. The Hoard's here, thanks to Ali's initiative. We've just checked."

"Anyway—" continued Martin, but Dr. West came even closer.

"Stop asking questions," he hissed. "Just shut up."

"Leave him, Dad," pleaded Eric. "Don't do anything we're going to regret . . ." His voice trailed away.

"What will you do with the Hoard now?" Martin persisted.

"We're taking it to Colsay," Eric replied quickly before his father could speak. "It's an island to the east. It used to be owned by our family."

"I shall keep it there," agreed Dr. West. "Where it belongs."

"Let's take them back first, Dad," said Eric urgently. "Martin can keep quiet. Martin can—"

Dr. West laughed. "What sort of fool do you take me for?" he said. "They've been lost at sea, haven't they? In the storm."

"What are you going to do?" asked Eric incredulously.

"The grotto," he said softly. "Both of them. I can manage Ali, Eric. You take care of the boy."

With casual ease Dr. West picked up Ali, who mumbled: "I won't miss the *Poznań*?"

"No," said Dr. West. "I'm taking you to the *Poznań* now."

"I'm not going anywhere," said Martin, scrambling to his feet.

Eric stared at his father blankly and then looked away, his lips working but no sound coming out. Then to Martin's complete surprise Eric rushed at him and they fell to the ground. As Eric pinned him down, he said, "My father's had a breakdown. Do as he says, or he'll kill us all."

Martin subsided. "I don't believe you," he whispered.

"You will," replied Eric, his eyes full of terror. "It's been coming for a long time."

Dr. West carried Ali lightly and gently as he scrambled precariously over the ridge of rocks that led around the corner of the cove. The sea was still choppy and, as they stumbled on, Martin could hear the hollow booming of surf.

"He really means to kill us?" whispered Martin.

"Dad's been obsessed with the Hoard ever since I was a kid," whispered Eric. "It's true our ancestors lived in Settler, but so did Magnus's. Anyway, he still felt the Hoard belonged to us, that it shouldn't be in the museum. But he's ill, Martin. I've seen it coming on, but I couldn't stop the illness. I do love him, but I can't help him. I realized he'd taken the stuff only quite recently. I've been trying to talk it out with him. But he's become worse. Day by day. And he keeps getting—" He broke off suddenly and turned away.

"What are we going to do?" Martin asked. "He can keep the Hoard for all I care. Can't we jump him? The two of us."

"No. He's terribly strong."

"So that's it. You'll let him kill us?" Martin sneered.

But Eric suddenly seemed to grow calmer. It's like the eye of the storm again, thought Martin. A very temporary calm.

"No," Eric replied. "There's a way out of the grotto. He doesn't know it. I do. It's a kind of funnel at the back. It goes up to the cliff top."

"Ali would never make it."

"You can pull him up—beyond the tide line," whispered Eric pleadingly.

"Thanks a lot," said Martin sarcastically.

"If you start trouble now, he'll kill us all."

"You as well?"

"Dad doesn't know what he's doing—he's ill," Eric repeated, angry now. "Can't you understand?"

"Why didn't you stop all this before it got going?"

"I didn't realize how it was. And he gave me the knife as a present. There's something about it. I wanted it so much."

"So it's got you too."

"What?"

"The Hoard. There must be some kind of spell on it."

"Nonsense."

"What are you whispering about, Eric?" Dr. West was suspicious.

"I was telling Martin that—what—had to be done—had to be done."

"Concentrate on what we're doing."

They were climbing down now while the cruel black cliff face soared above them. There were hundreds of gulls' nests, and Martin could feel little gimlet eyes upon them. They were invading another kingdom, and were unwelcome. The waves lashed and foamed below, curling at their feet, trying to draw them into the boiling sea.

Eventually they reached a cave. A rush of water hurled itself inside to collide in a hollow boom of spray with slimy rock and then to recoil, its tail hitting the next crest with a roar of frustration. The tide will come right up, thought Martin, the panic rising inside him. He really can't mean to leave us here. Then, to his horror, he saw Dr. West gently and carefully lay Ali on a ledge and produce a length of cord from his jacket pocket. Eric hadn't bargained on this, Martin thought, his heart beating wildly against his ribs.

"No, Dad."

"If I don't, they'll escape. And anyway, the sea will take them. They'll be part of the islands."

"You'll kill them, Dad."

"That isn't important," Dr. West replied gently.

"Aren't *I* important?"

"You're my son." Dr. West stared at Eric as if he had said something out of place.

"I'm staying. If you tie them up, I'm staying with them."

"Don't be a fool," said Dr. West dismissively. "They *must* be tied up."

Eric's frustration and despair suddenly boiled over, and he lunged wildly at his father, but Dr. West easily fended him off. For a moment he looked at Eric sadly and then chopped him hard on the back of the neck. Eric went down immediately and his father caught him, holding him lovingly to him for a few seconds. He caressed his hair and then placed him, as gently as he had Ali, on the seaweed-covered ledge. Slowly, with the cord held out, Dr. West approached Martin. There seemed to be no point in putting up a struggle. A few minutes later, having securely tied Martin's hands and ankles, Dr. West left, carrying Eric like a baby in his arms.

Eight

Martin felt completely unreal as he lay there, the cord biting into him viciously. Everything had happened so quickly that he could hardly take any of it in. This was the third time in twenty-four hours that he had faced death, and he just couldn't fight the shock of it again. Then he noticed something. Dr. West hadn't tied up Ali. Perhaps there hadn't been enough cord; perhaps he felt there was no need—that Ali was too far gone to make any attempt at escape. Maybe he was right; Ali lay on the ledge, his breathing less noisy, but he was certainly unconscious again.

Meanwhile, the water level was growing higher, and Martin realized with the same kind of numb acceptance that quite soon the cave would be full to the roof. He thought about this for a while, while the waves splashed icily onto his skin. Then, abruptly, the numbness disappeared and a great surge of panic swept over him. Martin began to struggle frantically, but the more he pulled, the deeper his bonds bit into him. He stopped, knowing it was all hopeless, that he was going to drown, and that it was going to be a terrifying ordeal.

Then he heard Ali mumble something, and his return to at least some kind of consciousness gave Martin a sudden joyous hope. After a few seconds Ali's muttering became a frantic, continuous plea. "It mustn't go without me. It mustn't go without me." He repeated the phrase over and over again, until his voice became less blurred, and with considerable effort he rolled over, half turning to Martin as he did so.

"He paid me."

"What?"

"He paid me, didn't he? Dr. West. He gave me the money. So I can catch the ship."

Martin had to think very fast. As he did so, an intense desire to survive grew in him.

"Ali—"

"Yes?"

"He gave me the money—to keep for you."

"Thank the good Lord for that." His relief made Martin realize how criminal his lie was. But he *had* to get Ali's assistance, however feeble that might be.

"You'll be able to help your family now."

"And the ship?"

"It's waiting for you. All you have to do is to help me."

The lie was easier now, particularly as the waves were splashing into Martin's face.

"Can't move," Ali said weakly.

"You just have." Martin was accusing.

"Dr. West. He'll help us."

"He's not here," he replied bleakly.

"He'll help us," persisted Ali doggedly.

"No. There's been—an accident," Martin said fiercely.

"Mmm." Ali seemed to be relapsing into sleep again.

"Ali, unless you help me, you'll miss the sailing."

"No." He clearly wasn't taking anything in.

"You *have* to help me."

By now the water had crept around Martin's waist. It was icy and strong, pulling at him, trying to wash him away.

"You have to help me *quickly*," he yelled.

"Sick," muttered Ali.

"Sick or not, you idiot. If you don't *do* something, you'll never see Africa again."

"What do you want?" He stirred again.

"I'm tied up, and the tide's coming in."

"Where's the money?" Ali mumbled with slightly more clarity.

"*I've* got the money," Martin repeated. "Dr. West gave it to me because you were sick. So if you don't help me, you won't have *anything* for your family. They'll die. All of them." He was compounding the lies, but it didn't matter. He could explain everything—straighten everything out—if only he could live, if only Ali could help him to live. The water roared again, creeping, clutching, its icy spray covering his face.

"Ali."

"What can I do?" He seemed slightly more positive this time.

"Get up. Untie me. Now."

"Sick."

He seemed to be giving up all over again, and Martin yelled at him: "Ali!"

"I'll try," he replied reluctantly.

"That's better. Try hard."

Martin watched Ali sit up slowly and painfully. He was obviously trying hard now to force his limbs into action. Meanwhile, the sea tore at Martin again with a roar.

With difficulty Ali levered himself off the ledge

and, breathing harshly, he almost fell into the water. But he regained his balance and edged his way toward Martin.

"Hurry."

"Coming." But he was very slow and his breathing was labored.

"Think of your family."

"Coming."

"The money."

"Coming." Ali continued to mutter.

"The ship. What's its name?"

"*Poznań*."

"You'll be on it. If we can get out."

"*Poznań*."

"Yes, there's not much time."

The water was well above his waist now. We've got no boat, he thought as Ali reached him, no way to escape from the island. And we're at Dr. West's mercy if he comes back. But at least we'll be out of here.

"My wrists. They're tied to my ankles."

As Ali began to fumble with exasperating slowness, the sea seemed to grow more ferocious, as if it didn't want to be deprived of him, and he swallowed a mouthful of briny water.

"Get *on* with it."

"Trying."

"Hurry!"

Ali fumbled uselessly.

"Come on."

"Can't manage."

"You *must*."

Martin could feel Ali's fingers on the knot. "That's it."

He fumbled again. "Wet."

"Get *on* with it."

At last Ali seemed to get more purchase on the cord. He tugged and pulled, the water rose, lapping at Martin's shoulders.

"For God's sake—"

"Trying."

"Try harder."

"Yes."

"Now!" The sea lashed into Martin's mouth again and he began to choke.

Ali's fingers were strong now, and Martin felt the knot loosen and then unravel. But his feet were still tied and his own fingers were too numb to help.

"You'll have to get under the water."

"I can't—" said Ali hopelessly.

"You must." More water poured into Martin's mouth, and he choked again.

"I'll try."

"Do that."

Ali tried again, dipping his head in and out of the flooding tide while he tore at the cord that seemed to grow tighter.

"Ali—I'm drowning!" bellowed Martin, choking and gasping again as the water poured over him.

"It's coming," said Ali doggedly.

"It's not."

"It is!"

And it was. Suddenly, gloriously, Martin was standing up. He threw his arms around Ali and they both fell into the frothing water.

Martin lugged and pulled a wheezing Ali out of the clawing tumult and somehow managed to drag him onto the slippery ledge. Ali lay there, exhausted and gasping, but the water was already creeping up toward them as each successive wave lashed its way in, making a demonic, hollow sound, like the plaintive howling of some underground creature.

"We've got to get out," said Martin.

"Sleep."

"No. There's a funnel—a chimney—that'll get us to the top of the cliffs." Martin tugged urgently at Ali's arm.

"Sleep."

"Later"

"Sick."

"You've got to make it."

With an enormous effort Ali pulled himself up.

"It's somewhere at the back. Hang on." Martin felt along the ledge. "Yes, it's here. It's going to be a very tight squeeze. Come on."

Ali struggled unwillingly to his feet and walked slowly over to Martin while the sea boomed and boomed again.

"It's narrow."

"I can't climb. My chest hurts."

"You'll have to. Follow me."

The chimney was very narrow indeed, but there were enough footholds to get a purchase.

"Are you okay?"

"Trying."

"Try harder." Martin knew that he had to be tough on him or he would give up. Would the sea pursue them? Maybe—it was thundering hard enough below.

The chimney curved sharply, but they continued to climb until it straightened out. Martin leaned back against the damp rock and shouted with joy and relief.

"What's happening?" wheezed Ali.

"I can see light."

"How far?"

"It's a long way. But we can do it, Ali. We can do it."

"Not sure."

"Course we can. We both can. You're going to catch the ship. . . ." Martin's voice faded out as he realized the true bleakness of what he really had to tell Ali, that the ship had probably gone, that there was no money, that they couldn't get off the island, and if they did, he would probably be arrested. Meanwhile, somewhere out there was the mad Dr. West. "Come on," he said, looking up toward the blessed light. Suddenly that was all that mattered.

The climb was relentlessly slow, but gradually they inched their way up, although Ali kept stopping, gasping and wheezing, saying he couldn't go on. But somehow, in his desperation, Martin always managed to get him going again. On and on they went, until the pale light became more intense.

"You okay?"

"Not okay."

"Almost there."

"You must give me the money."

"When we're up."

Minutes later they were at the top and Martin was helping to haul Ali out of the narrow opening to the chimney. Then they both collapsed on the wind-scarred peat and lay there. But they were free—and Martin had never felt so elated in his life. He pressed his face into the salty earth and wept with relief.

Eventually he sat up. He was stiff and cold but still wonderfully overjoyed to be alive. Gradually, he tried to come to grips with the next move. He might as well tell Ali now that everything he wanted— everything that Martin had guaranteed—was gone. He had to tell him now. Then he saw him, lying stretched out, gasping for breath. He couldn't tell him. Not now. It would kill him. He looked desperately around him. What could he do? It all seemed quite hopeless, but for Martin nothing could destroy the joy of being alive after all the dreadful things that had happened since Ali had kidnapped him.

"Where's the knife?" asked Martin, suddenly reminded of its existence.

"In the boat."

Then it was gone, he thought. It had been washed away in the storm, or it was with Dr. West.

"Where's the money?" returned Ali with terrible persistence.

"Down in the cove. I hid it."

"We must get down there now. The *Poznań* will leave without me."

"No, it won't. It's not due to go yet."

"What's the time?" Ali wheezed in agitated suspicion.

"It's all right," comforted Martin. "It really is all right."

Eager for any sign of hope—or even distraction—he peered down into the cove and saw a boat pulled up high on the beach with someone standing beside it. Seconds later, he realized he was looking at Magnus.

"Where you going?"

"Magnus is here."

"Don't go."

"Why?"

"He'll kill us."

"All right." Martin wanted to placate him. "I'll be careful. Let me go and see what he's up to."

"Be careful."

"I will."

There's a bond between us now, thought Martin. A real bond. Somehow he knew that it would last forever, even if they never saw each other again.

Magnus was his only hope—and Martin knew it. He was sure that he was innocent, but he still had to be careful, just in case. There had been so much conspiracy going on that he just didn't know—couldn't be certain about anyone or anything.

Martin ran on, down the rocky descent, and as he was scrambling over the last outcrop to the cove he met Magnus scrambling up.

Martin froze and Magnus stared back at him uneasily. For once he looked indecisive, and the

Viking grandeur of his features and physique seemed diminished. He looks like an old man, thought Martin, but beside him he still felt small, vulnerable. They were both standing on a wide, slippery rock that overlooked the groaning sea far below, and this made Martin feel even more insecure.

"Martin." He sounded exhausted.

"What are you doing here?" asked Martin hesitantly.

"Your parents. They're out of their minds with worry. Thank God I've found you."

"Where are they?"

"There's a full-scale search of the islands. Your dad and mom are with the lifeboat crew."

"And you?"

"On my own. The *Saturn*'s broken up, but we hoped that you and the African boy had managed to escape."

"Yes. But he's ill," said Martin guardedly.

"Are you all right?"

"I'm fine."

"Where is he?"

"Up there."

"Let's go."

"Wait." Martin knew that every moment could count for Ali. He'd taken a dreadful beating and could catch pneumonia—if he hadn't gotten it already. But he had to tell Magnus what had happened. Judge his reaction. "Dr. West's been here — with Eric."

"God—"

"He tried to drown us. And he's got the Hoard." An odd expression crossed Magnus's face. "He stole it from the museum," Martin added.

"I always suspected he did," snapped Magnus, "but I never had any proof. I scoured the island for it. Never found a trace. Lately, though, when there was talk of a figure in a cat mask at Settler, I had a feeling it must be there. I suppose it was Eric trying to scare people away. Pathetic."

"He scared me."

"He would have scared anyone down at Settler," said Magnus hurriedly, as if he were trying to appease him. "It's a strange place — brings out the fear in everyone. And then there was the legend about the witch cat to back it all up. I've been watching William West for a long time now, trying to fathom what he's been up to."

"Did you suspect the *Saturn?*" Martin asked thoughtfully.

"Yes, that's why I came down the night of the party. I'd seen him on the *Saturn* at Lerwick. They didn't know what they were taking on." He paused.

"You were scared of me, weren't you, Martin?"

"I thought you'd taken it."

"So did my boy Peter. Eric told him I had."

"Was that the reason for the fight?" asked Martin, shivering.

"Probably. But Eric was only playing games. He didn't realize his father's financial problems—the problems that finally broke him."

"What are they?"

"He embezzled money from the chamber of commerce. He's their treasurer."

"But why on earth should he suddenly do that?"

"I don't know. I don't know what was driving him. But whatever it was, it tipped him over the edge." He paused. "Do you trust me now? I want you to trust me before we help Ali."

"I trust you," said Martin, though a shred of apprehension still remained.

Magnus put his arm around Martin. "Let's get back to him then," he said.

"He *is* bad." Magnus and Martin were kneeling down beside Ali, whose breathing had become stentorian again. "He needs to be hospitalized. Right away."

"How bad?"

"I don't know. But he needs help immediately."

"What can we do?" Martin felt deeply afraid for Ali. Whatever Ali had done, they had a bond all right. They *must* save him.

"I'll radio from my boat—and the helicopter can intercept us."

"How do we get him down?"

"Any more blankets? There's a store here, isn't there?"

"I've used most of them," said Martin.

"Use whatever's left. Wrap him tightly." Magnus spoke quickly and decisively. "I'll go back and get on the radio fast. Then I'll come straight back with that stove you've got on the beach."

"Magnus . . ." Martin was hesitant.

"Yes?"

"I can trust you, can't I?"

Magnus put a hand on his arm. "Yes. I promise you can. Now go for those blankets. Quick."

Magnus appeared not long after Martin had finished wrapping Ali in the blankets.

"Did you expect to see me back?" he asked quietly.

"Yes, I told you. I trust you. Did you get through?" Suddenly, despite the joy of his escape, Martin was exhausted.

"The helicopter should be here in about twenty minutes." Magnus looked down at Ali and then up at Martin. "You've done well," he said. His eyes were warm and encouraging. Magnus had almost returned to his old charismatic self. "We just need to keep him warm, and try to get some soup down him. I've brought the stove up."

"I tried to give him some baked beans earlier on," gabbled Martin.

Magnus smiled. "It'd be hard for him to swallow those with that fever," he said. "But don't worry, you've done a wonderful job. You've kept Ali alive in the most appalling situation." He lit the stove and began to open the can of soup. "He'll be all right—he'll make it now." Magnus sounded very reassuring.

Martin looked at Ali anxiously. He knew there was a long way to go before they could really be sure that Ali had been saved.

Ten minutes later the weather began to clear and the sea to calm slightly. It was afternoon, and the sun swept Filla with a faint, melancholic warmth. Martin lay back, basking in the unexpected heat. He felt relaxed and even his damp clothing seemed bearable. Ali's breathing was easier now and Magnus's words rang in his ears: "He'll make it now." Maybe he would after all.

Magnus sat next to Ali, looking solidly confident. He had made Martin drink some of the soup and found another rather ragged blanket at the back of the store for him.

"Where's Colsay?" Martin asked.

"Not very far. You can see it from here."

"What's it like?"

"Much the same as Filla, except there's an old Viking settlement on it."

"Where exactly is it?" He sat up and stared out over the calming sea.

"There's a bit of mist out there," said Magnus. "But you can see the peak."

He could—a crag emerging from what looked like cotton.

"There's something out there," said Martin.

"You've got younger eyes—what is it?" Magnus's voice was sharp.

"Hang on. It's coming out of the mist now. It—it looks like a klondyker."

"Couldn't be. Not out here. These aren't fishing grounds, and there's a damn nasty reef."

"I thought it was, Magnus. It certainly looked like a klondyker. But maybe it was a trick of the mist." Martin turned to look eagerly at Magnus, but he didn't seem very interested. He was fiddling with the stove and it was with some surprise and a little alarm that Martin saw one of his hands was shaking.

The helicopter arrived almost exactly on time and

a man was winched down while the chattering machine hovered overhead. He had an armband that read PARAMEDIC and he examined Ali quickly with a stethoscope.

"We'll take him to Lerwick," he said briskly.

"Is he going to be all right?" asked Martin anxiously.

"I hope so. He's very ill, but they have a brilliant team at Aberdeen. They'll do everything they can for him."

He signaled down a stretcher on a couple of lines and within minutes Ali was strapped on and about to be winched up.

"You must go with them, Martin. You should have a full checkup," said Magnus.

"No, I'm fine. I want to go back to Mom and Dad and Clare."

"I haven't got time to take him there," said the paramedic. "Either he comes with us to Lerwick or he stays with you, sir. Personally, I think he should come with us."

"No," said Martin. "No way. I must go home."

The paramedic shrugged. "I have to get this patient to Lerwick. Fast. I haven't got time to hang around."

"I'll take care of him," said Magnus.

Ali opened his eyes as the stretcher began to lift.

"Where's the money?" he managed to get out. "Where's the boat?"

Martin tried and failed to think of something to say; he could hear Ali repeating the questions over and over again as he traveled skyward.

"More soup?" asked Magnus solicitously.

"Thanks."

"We'll start moving when you've finished this. Now that Ali's on his way."

But Martin noticed Magnus wasn't watching the rescue helicopter as it became a speck in the distance. Instead, he was staring out toward the horizon. He followed Magnus's eyes and saw the klondyker again. It was much nearer this time.

"I'm right. It *is* a klondyker."

"Looks like it," he replied reluctantly. "I've got some binoculars in the boat—but yes, I'm pretty sure." Magnus's voice was suddenly brittle and tense.

"Why are they coming in here?" asked Martin.

"All the ships in the area have been scouring the seas for you and Ali. I expect the helicopter's passed on the news about you both. Maybe they haven't been told that Ali is on his way to Lerwick." Magnus spoke rapidly and Martin could see his hands were shaking again.

"Let's go down to the beach and wait for them. Be

better to travel back on it than in a small boat again." Martin felt all his anxiety returning.

"They won't send a boat ashore for a while. Sit quietly and drink your soup." Magnus tried to sound casual.

"But we could light the fire again." said Martin. He knew he must do something—get busy. "They might not know where to land, and the cove is the only place, isn't it?"

"Well . . ." Magnus seemed curiously reluctant to commit himself.

"What's the matter?" Martin turned slowly around to face him.

Magnus sighed. "You should have gone in the helicopter." He put his head in his hands. "I ought to make a move now, but I'm so damned tired."

"What's the matter?"

"Nothing."

"Come on," urged Martin. "There *is* something, isn't there? What is it?" The sun was not so hot now, or at least it didn't seem to be. Martin gave an involuntary shiver. It was all going wrong again—or was it simply his battered reactions playing on his imagination? He hoped to God it was just that.

"Let's get that fire going again," said Magnus with sudden decision.

Nine

Once on the beach, with two of them working on it, they were soon able to make the fire flare up again. Magnus seemed to have an eagle eye for bits of driftwood, and he climbed agilely from rock to rock, extracting bits and pieces from the most unlikely crevices. They worked together silently and companionably while the klondyker edged silently nearer. Eventually it anchored about a hundred yards off the reef and Martin watched a dinghy being winched down. Squinting, he saw two men, one at the outboard and the other sitting in the prow, staring ahead at the crackling flames.

The sun had set now behind dark clouds, but there was no hint of wind. As the boat drew nearer, Martin recognized one of the men in the boat.

"It's Captain Kinlata," he said excitedly. "That must be the *Poznań*, then."

Magnus stood on the rocks, saying nothing,

doing nothing. He seemed curiously inanimate.

"It's Captain Kinlata," repeated Martin, staring up at him, puzzled.

"Yes," said Magnus quietly. "I can see him now." There was something incredibly bleak in the tone of his voice.

"Good afternoon." The captain jumped out onto the beach, followed by his companion, who, to Martin's surprise, was quite young. He was wearing a sweater, jeans, and a denim jacket, and looked completely out of place.

"Are you Martin Fuller?" he asked formally.

Something began to form in Martin's mind—an answer, a conclusion that he still couldn't understand, although he felt it was on the tip of his tongue. "Yes, I'm Martin Fuller and this is Magnus Dunglas."

"Were you with Ali?" interrupted Captain Kinlata. "They say he's ill, in a cave—a message came through . . ."

"He's gone to Lerwick in the helicopter," said Martin. Briefly he told them the whole story and they listened carefully.

As he was talking, Martin wondered why Magnus was remaining so silent. But before he could turn to him, the young man in the denim jacket said,

"You've certainly been through an ordeal." He looked at Martin with a kind of impatient respect, but Captain Kinlata was defensive.

"I had no idea what he had on board the *Saturn*," he said. "Using the Lada, too."

"You're going to have a tough job proving that," replied the young man sharply, and the captain looked very worried indeed.

"Dr. West and Mr. Dunglas here have always been so welcoming. It's been special for us—coming here," he said, speaking very quickly. "Dr. West gave me that car, for instance. It wasn't worth anything, he said, wouldn't fetch much if he sold it."

"He deceived you," said Martin. "Like he deceived all of us."

The young man looked skeptical. "That remains to be seen," he said crisply.

Then Magnus spoke for the first time. "May I ask who you are?"

"Detective Inspector Tomlinson. I've been interviewing Captain Kinlata. Some members of his crew told us that this boy, Ali, had taken you away in one of the *Saturn*'s dinghies, and that he was also carrying a number of boxes. But Captain Kinlata claims that's all he knows," he finished irritably, as if he suspected Captain Kinlata of knowing far more than he had told him.

"Yes," replied Magnus, and Martin stared at him, wondering at his flat, expressionless voice.

"Have you any comment, Mr. Dunglas?" asked Tomlinson.

"No," said Magnus, and Martin stared at him in amazement. He looked weird—zombielike. What was happening to him?

There was a short, very tense silence. Then Tomlinson continued rapidly, officiously. "One of the police boats in the search noticed a small craft making for Colsay about forty minutes ago. They boarded, and questioned a Dr. West and his son. The boy didn't say much at first—seemed half asleep—but just as my officers were about to disembark, the boy broke down and said that there were two people in danger of death on Filla. He was able to give a very accurate description of their whereabouts, but his father remained absolutely silent. I was contacted immediately on the *Poznań* so that I could investigate while Dr. West and his son were further questioned." Tomlinson paused and stared at Magnus. Then he continued slowly, "I was told the boy had some complicated story about stolen antiques. Seems to tie up with some of the things *you've* just told me."

"Did Dr. West have nothing to say?" asked Magnus casually.

"Nothing, but he was clearly either ill, or deeply distressed in some way."

"*Distressed!*" said Martin in disgust. "He's mad — nearly did Ali and me in."

Tomlinson turned to Magnus. "Eric West made some very serious allegations against you, sir. I shall have to ask you to come with me for questioning."

"What allegations? What did Eric say?" Martin's words fell over one another. He didn't think he could bear any more uncertainty.

"Eric West alleges his father and Mr. Dunglas here were partners in a scheme to rebuild and repopulate a small village on the island. To finance this, ten years ago they stole some valuable antiquities and hid them with a view to sell them at a later date."

"*You*—you lied to me, told me . . ." Martin's voice trailed away as Magnus interrupted savagely.

"No one will ever understand what Settler means to us. The whole of Shetland could have been regenerated, with the people living in the old way—the good way—close to the sea and soil. Dependent on their hands, in tune with the elements. It was our dream and it became an obsession. Poor William— couldn't take the strain of the theft—the fact that the Hoard was buried in Settler. It gradually broke him, the waiting and the tension and the enormity of what we had done."

"You realize that anything you say will be taken down and—"

"I realize that."

"Why?" asked Martin. "*Why* does it mean so much to you both?"

Magnus spoke slowly, weighing every word, anxious that they should somehow understand. "William West and I represent two of the oldest families on Shetland and that means more than anything in the world to us. We both originated from the Settler community. A few ruined crofts might seem nothing to you, but they were all-important to us. Of course, they were so-called cursed, but we could undo that with the Hoard money. The theft, the waiting we hadn't calculated on, the realization that they were too well-known to sell immediately, that's what broke West. Split our families. Even Peter and Eric became locked in a contest for the silver knife. But using Ali was one of the worst things we did. I'd met him through Captain Kinlata, realized how naive he was, understood how desperate he was about his family, and used him." Magnus was silent. "But things went wrong," he continued, "and William—well—you know what he was driven to."

"How could you use me like that, Magnus?" Martin burst out. "All those lies. I suppose planting the knife in my saddlebag was the only way you had of ensuring Ali would come after me in your van and get me out of the way until the boxes had been transferred. You must have told him I'd show it to my parents, say the rest of the stuff was probably on the *Saturn* in the car, and he wouldn't get his money. I know he wouldn't have agreed to attack me like that otherwise. And it got the knife away from Eric. He was getting too careless for you, wasn't he? But you didn't want Peter to fight with him for it or appear to have taken it yourself. Even today, still keeping up the pretense, lying to me," Martin repeated bitterly. "I thought you were our friend, but it was Ali who protected me, and Eric—"

"You'll never know how much it hurt me to deceive you, Martin. I suppose I was obsessed too—as much as William was."

"Was it so important to rebuild Settler?" asked Martin curiously, some of his anger draining away. He couldn't work out whether Magnus was telling the truth or pumping out another stream of lies. But somehow he didn't feel it was just greed that had motivated him.

"Yes. It was of paramount importance to us to bring it back to life. For our families."

"Would it have cost all that money—all the Hoard money?"

"To turn it into a working community—easily. And we wanted to invest the money as well, to ensure the future of the settlement."

"I don't believe you," said Tomlinson. "All this for a few old crofts."

"They're magical," said Magnus. "We had a chance of living in the old way again."

"I can understand that," said Captain Kinlata unexpectedly. "It would be much the same in our country. Old ways are essential." He turned to Martin. "Will Ali live?" he asked abruptly.

"They seemed to think he had a good chance," replied Martin, looking worried.

"I must radio the hospital," Kinlata said, turning back to the dinghy.

"Wait," said Tomlinson brusquely. "We'll take these two with us and then sail back to Lerwick, if the *Poznań* captain agrees—and he'll have to—" He walked a few steps up the beach. "Magnus Dunglas. I am arresting you on a preliminary charge of stealing antiquities. I want you to . . ."

But suddenly Magnus turned his back on him and began to scramble over the rocks. He was so quick that he caught them all off guard.

"Don't run off on me!" shouted Tomlinson. "You don't stand a chance."

But Magnus didn't reply. He had reached the cliff now and was beginning to climb.

"Don't" shouted Martin suddenly. "Don't— Magnus."

Magnus turned a corner on the rocky promontory and disappeared from sight. Tomlinson raced off in pursuit and began to climb after him. They seemed well matched: Magnus surefooted and experienced; Tomlinson young and athletic.

"Martin," snapped Captain Kinlata. But Martin had gone.

Magnus wove his way along the lower part of the cliffs while Tomlinson followed and Martin brought up the rear. In front, the two men paced each other, neither gaining an inch as they leapt from rock to rock. Martin, hampered by his damp clothes and lack of fitness and experience in rock-scrambling, was falling farther and farther behind. He kept looking up at the gathering black clouds. Was it rain? Another storm? Simply a brooding sky? The weather was beginning to matter a very great deal for a reason he couldn't figure out. Maybe it was so much a part of the island that it governed his mood, all their moods.

As Martin pounded on, he was determined that Magnus would not take his own life, for he was sure that that was what he intended to do. And he understood why; he realized now that he had understood why the very first time he had stood among the ruined crofts at Settler. There had definitely been an old magic in that place, and when the sun shone, there was an ancient sunlight. Surely Settler was cursed only by its people leaving; it was waiting to be settled again. He had felt the very land itself warm to his own footsteps, and he could see why Magnus and Dr. West had stolen for it. But the hope of reawakening Settler had been too much for both of them. It had driven Dr. West dangerously mad—and was even now driving Magnus to his death. They had wanted old magic and ancient sunlight, but it had always been beyond their reach because it couldn't be re-created.

Martin suddenly caught sight of them. Magnus had begun to run down toward a huge granite slab, black and towering over the mounting sea, like a fortress, forbidding and treacherous. He disappeared behind it, followed by Tomlinson. Martin raced to join them, but before he could catch up with them he heard a sharp cry. When he rounded the slab, he saw Tomlinson on a ledge looking down, and Magnus's head was bobbing up and down on the creamy surface of the swirling water. When Martin joined Tomlinson he found he was looking down into a gully that was filled with rushing water. Magnus was swimming toward it—and the open sea.

"Magnus," yelled Martin.

"I'll go in after him." Tomlinson was pulling off his shoes.

"Wait, you'll both drown. Just wait. Magnus! Magnus please!" Martin ran along the ledge as far as he could go. "Don't go out there. We can still have Settler."

"*We?*" he shouted, turning on his back for a moment and treading water.

"Me and Peter and Eric and you—"

"I'll be in prison."

"Not forever."

"I'm sixty." He turned to his front and began to swim out again.

"What about Peter?"

Still he swam on, nearing the gully now—and the open sea.

"Peter," yelled Martin. He'd come to the end of the ledge. "What about Peter?"

There was a slight hesitation in Magnus's stroke.

"You can't leave him. He feels the same way about Settler. And Eric and his mother will be alone."

Magnus turned on his back again.

"What good can I do? In prison."

"We'll all fight for you."

"I stole a national treasure."

"That's all I can say—we'll fight for you."

"Martin, you'll have left Shetland, you'll forget."

"I'll never forget—and I'll come back." Martin spoke with conviction.

With sudden decision Magnus turned, and with great floundering strokes tried to swim back to the rock face. But he seemed to have no strength left, and the more he swam, the more the tide pulled him toward the sea.

"Stay here," said Tomlinson, throwing off his denim jacket and diving off the ledge. Without even thinking, Martin followed.

The water was icy. Without even a fragile boat to protect him this time, Martin knew that he didn't have long before he'd seize up completely in the searing cold. The powerful swell caught them, but by swimming as hard as they could, Tomlinson and Martin fought themselves abreast of Magnus, who was hardly moving at all now—just floating and being carried forward by the tide.

"Grab him," spluttered Tomlinson. "Try and get him on his back."

The water pushed them forward as they struggled

with Magnus's inert body. Eventually they managed to turn him over, and they treaded water for a while, knowing they could never carry him back against the tide. Martin knew Magnus was trying to help them as much as he could, but they were making no progress whatsoever.

"Thank God," said Tomlinson suddenly.

"What?"

"Look—in front of us."

The tide was sweeping them onto a rocky bar with a narrow shingle beach.

Beyond the beach was white water breaking, but Martin knew they were going to make it. A few seconds later all three of them were wading in the shallows.

"That was meant," gasped Martin.

Magnus only smiled.

"I'm sure I'm right," insisted Martin. "The old magic."

"There isn't any," he breathed. "Settler isn't meant to be reawakened."

But Martin felt a surge of total conviction. "It is," he insisted. "It's waiting for us now."

"What the hell are you two talking about?" panted Tomlinson as he dragged himself to his feet. He looked at Martin. "Don't you understand—

between them, these villains could have killed you."

Looking out at the lashing surf, Martin was silent.

"Believe me," said Tomlinson. "They would just have left you."

Martin looked down at Magnus. "I'll never really know," he replied.

Epilogue

Five weeks later

Settler was once again inhabited—if only temporarily. Mr. and Mrs. Fuller, Clare, Peter, Eric, and Ali were sitting around a fire on the beach, where they were roasting potatoes. On a barbecue nearby, hamburgers and frankfurters grilled gently, giving out the most delicious smell. Martin sat a little apart, watching them, thinking—and they let him do this, knowing that was what he wanted.

The weather had changed. Fall had set in, and on this windless Sunday lunchtime, the sea and sky merged in cold gray steel. The crofts, open to the sky, their walls covered in lichen, seemed to stare out at them. There was a great stillness there—a feeling of eternity.

A good deal had happened since they had rescued Magnus from the Filla seas. Ali had recovered and was soon to be repatriated by his shipping company, the police having decided not to prosecute him.

Meanwhile, the Shetlanders had raised a considerable sum for him to take back to his family in Nigeria.

Dr. West was in a psychiatric hospital on the mainland, and the charges against him would be considered in the light of the doctor's report. Magnus, however, was in a remand prison in Aberdeen, although his lawyers had high hopes of a mitigated sentence because of his age and the many letters of support they had received from members of the community. So it doesn't all end cozily, thought Martin sadly. His mother got up from her place and brought him a cup of hot chocolate.

"No knockout drops in this one," she said, smiling at him.

"May I join you?" Ali stood beside them.

"Sure," said Martin. "I was just sitting here, thinking about it all."

"I can see why Magnus and Dr. West wanted this village so much," said Ali suddenly.

"You too?" Martin looked up at him with interest.

"I think they behaved very stupidly," said Mrs. Fuller firmly. "Two grown men plotting and planning—stealing—just to resurrect an old place like this. I mean, who would want to live here anyway? It's bleak and cold all year round."

Ali shook his head. "It's like my village back home—except mine is alive with people. It's not bleak and cold; it's very hot. But it is a tribe—a community. Like Settler was. I want to go back to my village. But I'll need some formal education, be a teacher, maybe. Get the village together."

"No one did that here," said Martin. "They just ran out on it."

"It could be gotten going again," replied Ali.

"Romantic nonsense," said Martin's mother.

Martin turned away. He didn't want to hear her opinion. His gaze fell on the *Saturn*, lying broken in two on the rocks. Its bow had risen up, dwarfing the crofts, and the stern had drifted back to lie upturned in deeper water. It was a tragic sight. Martin caught Ali's eye—he was looking at the ship sadly too.

"*It* was like a village—once you got used to it. It was hard, that life. But you made friends."

"Yes," said Martin. "You're right. They belong together—the klondyker and the crofts. Do you think they'll ever move it?"

"Maybe," said Ali. "But it'll be a tricky salvage job. They've stripped it of everything that can be moved out. So I think it'll be around for a while."

"That's good," said Martin. "They'll keep each other company."

"Your father was talking about a campaign they're starting to renovate the place—to have people living here again." Mrs. Fuller spoke impatiently and they knew she didn't approve.

Martin looked from the wreck of the klondyker and back to the roofless, ruined crofts again and thought of Eric's cat man keeping guard over Settler—and the Hoard. Martin smiled; maybe there would be a new community here one day. But for the moment Settler was alone with its ghosts. He picked up a piece of driftwood, pitted with holes from sandworms, and pressed it to his cheek. It was cold and salty and had the smell of Settler. For a moment he thought he saw smoke coming from a ruined chimney and imagined the crofters gathering around their peat fire while the gray ocean thundered outside. Then the mist began to roll in from the headland, covering Settler with a protective blanket.

"Come on," said his mother. "It's time to go home."

But Martin was at home where he was—here among the old magic of the weather-haunted ruins.

About the author

Anthony Masters lives in England, where he is highly acclaimed as a writer of novels for young readers. Although he often runs writing workshops in American schools, *A Watching Silence* is his first book for children to be published in the United States.